I0770916

RETRIBUTIONS

FRANK ARJUNE

Retributions

Copyright © [2025] by **Frank Arjune**

For permissions requests, contact:

Writersway Solutions, LLC

10685 Hazelhurst Dr STE B #38295

Houston, Texas, 77043, USA

www.writerswaysolutions.com

1-888-666-4258

Written and Illustrated by **Frank Arjune**

ISBN (Paperback): 978-1-962733-52-6

ISBN (Hardback): 978-1-962733-57-1

ISBN (Ebook): 978-1-962733-51-9

Printed in the United States of America

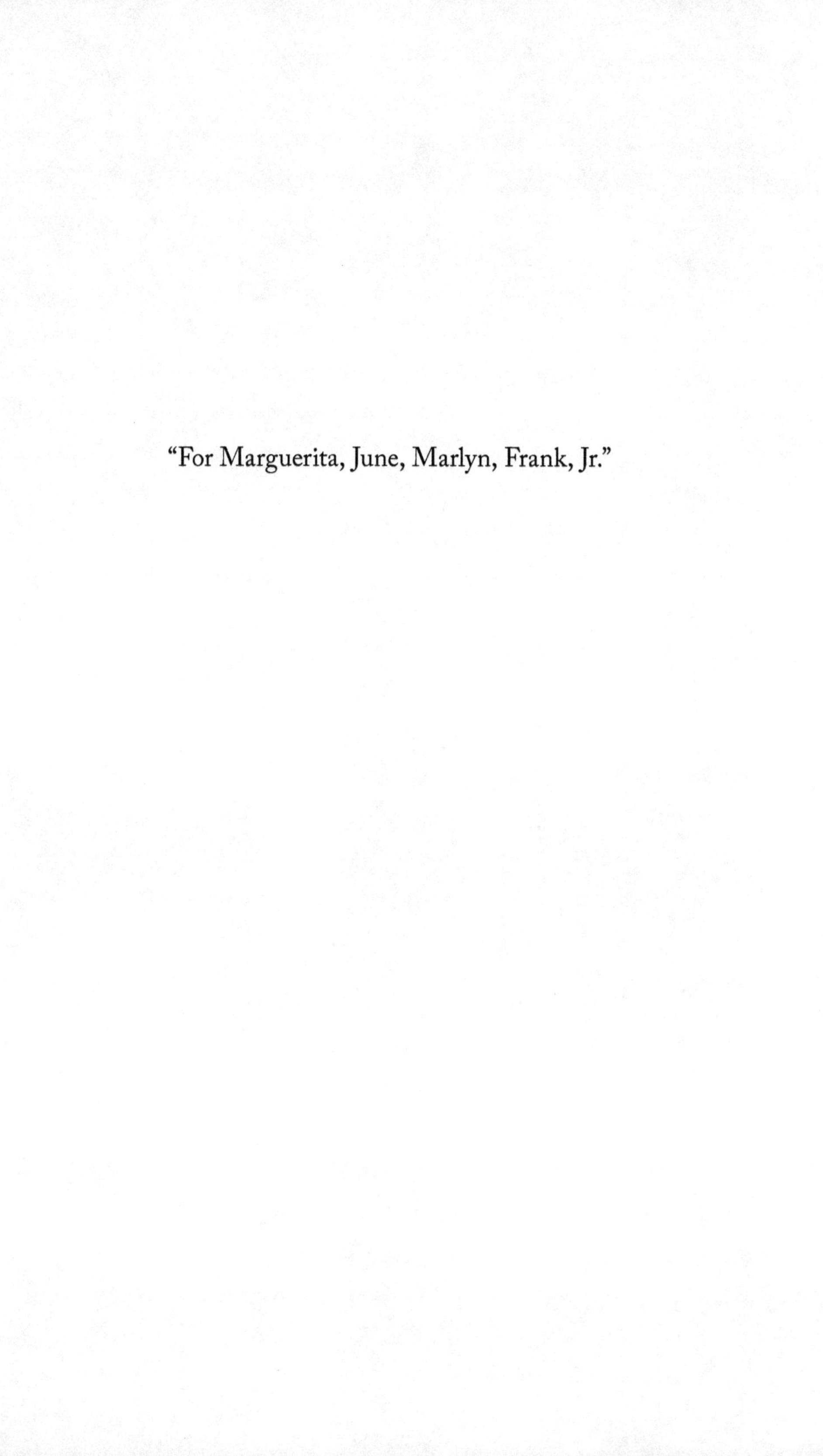

"For Marguerita, June, Marlyn, Frank, Jr."

ACKNOWLEDGMENT

I would like to give thanks to my nephew, Latchman, for inspiring me to write this story. I am grateful to my relatives, who allowed me to use their correct names. I am thankful to my wife, Marguerita, who unknowingly helped me, and to my typist, for consenting to type the manuscript.

The names have been changed where the author thought it was most appropriate. The names of the author's parents, elder sister, mother-in-law, and their children are correct and used with their mutual consent. The names of the author's younger brothers and sisters are all true and correct. All other names are fictional.

The author did not knowingly try to degrade or to disgrace any of the characters mentioned in this story. There are records in the police files and in the archives of the High Courts of Guyana pertaining to the death of Arjune of 126 Ocean View, Uitvlugt, West Coast Demerara, Republic of Guyana, South America.

1

The actions of men are universal. No matter what country or continent he was born in, man's basic instincts to survive, to protect his family, and to seek food, clothing, and shelter are intrinsically the same.

Baboo Arjune Dulamdin, a native of Guyana, on the mainland of South America, was determined to work hard, to have a large house, to send his eight children to school, and at the same time, to live a comfortable and a pleasurable life.

At age forty-six, Baboo Arjune was economically stable by working at two jobs. He worked at the Uitvlugt sugar factory as a supervisor of the millhouse, being the engineer and mechanic of the machinery at the sugar mill. During his time off, Baboo Arjune filled in his spare time by doing tailoring at home. He was a cutter, fitter, and tailor of boys' and men's clothing. He cut, fitted, and sewed undergarments, shirts, pants, farmer's overalls, security uniforms, waistcoats, and dress suits for boys and men, respectively. Baboo Arjune was ambidextrous and very competent. He worked at the factory at weekly shifts. The shifts ranged from 7:00 a.m. to 3:00 p.m., 3:00 p.m. to 12:00 midnight, and 12:00 midnight to 7:00 a.m.

When Baboo worked the first shift, he would return home by about 4:00 p.m. After a bath and a snack, Baboo would sit down at his sewing machine and work away until it was about midnight. When Baboo worked the second shift at the factory, he found more time to rest. He would go straight to bed after taking a quick bath. He would sleep until about 7:00 a.m., after which he would do his tailoring until about 2:00 p.m., when it was time for him to go to his regular job at the sugar factory.

Baboo would not spend much time on breakfast, lunches, or dinners. All meals were home-cooked either by his wife, Mangri, or by his eldest child present, at that time, at home.

During the 12:00 midnight to 7:00 a.m. shift, Baboo found the most spare time to do his tailoring. When he got home from work in the mornings, Baboo would relax for about two hours, because he could not sleep in the hot tropical weather during the day. On the coastland of West Demerara, where he resided, it would be about ninety-eight degrees. But this high temperature was fanned by the cooling winds from the Atlantic Ocean when the tide washes.

However, within the house, the searing heat of the sun would make the galvanized sheets of the roof oven hot. This heat, instead of rising beyond the outer roof, would also vent itself through the close-boarded inner roof of the house and would heat up the living and sleeping quarters of the house and make life sweaty, sticky, and uncomfortable when the water was falling in the Atlantic Ocean, that was only about one hundred yards away from Baboo's house.

Baboo, most times, at home, would be clad in a sleeveless cotton vest and a pair of khaki shorts. During the week of his third shift, he would begin working at his sewing machine, which was a Singer all-purpose machine, from about 10:00 a.m. until about 6:00 p.m. Baboo would achieve tremendous output during this particular week.

As he completed his pieces of clothing, he would toss them to Mangri, who would sit on the polished crabwood floor and do the hemming on the pants folds and sew on the buttons on all the garments, wherever they were needed. Mangri would thread her sewing needles with one, two, or three doubled threads, as the handwork necessitated. She would use beeswax on the threads. She worked neatly and diligently, putting on the finishing touches on the garments produced by Baboo. Mangri often complained of overworking. She cared for the children, cooked, washed, and helped with sewing on buttons and hand hemming pants folds.

Mangri and Baboo often quarreled, but the bottom line was that the job had to be done.

At age forty-six, Baboo was 6'2", weighed a hundred and eighty pounds, very light complexioned, with salt-and-pepper hair. He had brown eyes, wore a well-trimmed mustache, and had gold caps on his canine teeth. He would smile readily and would be angered only when he was constantly provoked. At these times, his straight nose would become red on his angular face. Baboo Arjune was of East Indian descent by birth, and an extremely handsome man.

On the other hand, Mangri was 5' tall, dark complexioned, with long straight black hair and an oval face. In 1967, Mangri was thirty-nine years old and the mother of eight children. Mangri was also of East Indian heritage, with ancestry, like Baboo Arjune, from India.

Both Baboo's and Mangri's parents were Indians and were brought to work on the sugar plantations as indentured laborers, replacing the freed African slaves on the Guyana cane lands. Indentureship was promulgated by the British government who saw the East Indians as a suitable labor force capable of working in the hot, tropical Guyana climate.

Mangri's father rose on the Plantation DeKinderen on the west coast of Demerara to be a sardar (i.e., a field foreman), and Baboo Arjune's father became known on Plantation Uitvlugt as Mahatoo (i.e., good and kind moneylender).

When Baboo was sixteen years old, he was married to Mangri, who was then nine. The marriage was arranged by the parents, who were popular residents on the two sugar plantations. The marriage was by common law, which was accepted then in the society. No legal documents or marriage license was issued to the parties in marriage, nor was the marriage legally recorded in the registry of marriages, births, and deaths.

After the common-law marriage had taken place, Mangri remained at her parents' home for two more years. At age eleven, Mangri was taken to her in-laws' home at Plantation Uitvlugt to live with her husband, Baboo, and his parents.

At age fourteen, Mangri gave birth to her first child, a son, who died at childbirth. From the time Mangri had entered the household of her in-laws, she became a grass cutter, joining her mother-in-law and father-in-law in the cane fields and in the irrigation canals among the fields to cut grass to feed the many heads of mulching cows that were reared by Dulamdin, Baboo's father.

Baboo was never allowed to cut grass, nor milch the cows. Baboo's parents took special care of him. He was given two pints of warm milk cream to enjoy each evening. His parents felt that because he was so light complexion, he would not have to soil himself by cutting grass or milching cows.

However, because of Mangri's dark skin color, Baboo's parents felt that she was fit for the fields, in particular, Baboo's mother and sisters. Baboo's father, on the other hand, loved and respected Mangri, whom he felt should be adored because she came from the elite class among the East Indians. Of course, Dulamdin reasoned, her father was a sardar!

Often, when the others were not paying attention, Dulamdin would steal the cream of the boiled milk and give it to Mangri. Mangri liked her father-in-law. She also loved Baboo, who was the apple in the eyes of his parents and of the village. The village women went after Baboo. Mangri was jealous, and many quarrels and fights ensued. As more and more children were born to the couple, Baboo began to mellow with age and became more industrious.

In the year 1967, Baboo's family had grown tremendously. There were five daughters and three sons born to the couple. The eldest child was Mona, who in the year 1967, was already married and was the mother of three children, two boys and a girl. The second child was also a daughter named Lena, who was also married and was the mother of two children. The other children, in consecutive order, were Frank, Margaret, Kenneth, Lynette, Jeanette, and Radhi. Radhi was the baby of the family and was born on May 6, 1960.

By the year 1967, Baboo Arjune was enjoying much prosperity through his arduous labor. His ambition was to earn money and to let his children have a sound education. Baboo Arjune dreamed of his children attending high school and then college. He wanted his children to be professionals, either teachers, engineers, lawyers, or doctors.

Baboo was conscious of the impact of education. As a plant foreman, through experience on the job, he was called upon to repair the sugar mill whenever it broke down, but Baboo was not adequately paid for what he did.

Baboo was embittered. Whenever he worked with his team of laborers at the millhouse, he was managed by the young men who were brought from England, Scotland, or Wales. Most times, when Baboo had problems repairing the sugar mills or making new parts for the machinery in the workshop of the factory, Baboo was given little or no assistance from his expatriate bosses. He fended for himself, with his fellow workers, and completed the repairs! But who reaped the benefits for the laborious task accomplished? Of course, the managers!

Baboo Arjune was determined that his children would not have to work as hard as he did. He knew that if his children were educated, they would be able to get white-collar jobs in the society and to live comfortable lives.

In 1967, Baboo Arjune was earning $180 per month as plant foreman. This money was inadequate to put enough food on the table. In order to make ends meet, to send his children to school, to purchase school uniforms, textbooks, and notebooks, Baboo labored on his sewing machine. He worked at home almost continuously, but he did not complain. He believed in "From the sweat of your brows you shall eat bread" and he enjoyed reaping the fruits of his labor.

In 1967, as the only breadwinner in his family, Baboo's income from both jobs sufficed. He was adequately able to take care of the needs of his family and also to save for a rainy day. His neighbors, who lived in very close proximity of his house, often saw Baboo burning the midnight lamp. They would often hear Baboo working at his sewing machine. His neighbors would see Mangri purchasing heaps of fish and shrimps from the mobile door-to-door fishmongers. The neighbors often saw Mangri purchasing large quantities of groceries.

His inquisitive neighbors saw Baboo Arjune entertaining his African friends with food and drinks at home.

In 1967. Baboo Arjune was independent. His tailoring had expanded, and his clientele had widened. Baboo had extended his home and had beautified his yard. By the time Lena was born in 1947, Baboo and Mangri had built and moved into their own house at 126 Ocean View, Uitvlugt.

In the year 1967, Baboo had extended this house twice. The first time was to add another bedroom and to enlarge the dining room and the sitting room. The second time was to enclose the bottom of the house, around the ten-foot concrete stilts, constructing an entirely new apartment for Mona, her husband, Hanuman, and her three children, to live.

Baboo's neighbors became extremely jealous. When Baboo was at the factory during the day and the children were at school, the neighborhood women would call out for Mangri. They would insult and curse her. They would challenge and threaten her. Mangri, who was also a proud woman, did not ignore the challenges. She often returned the insults and cursed back at those who tormented her.

The taunting and torments continued day after day. Mangri was often attacked when she walked the streets of her village. Many times Baboo received complaints from the neighborhood men about Mangri harassing their wives and daughters. Most times, Mangri was falsely accused for starting the neighborhood quarrels. Baboo warned Mangri to ignore the neighbors and to remain quiet.

Matters became worse as Baboo sewed at nights. Very often, huge stones would be hurled on the galvanized-sheeted roof of Baboo's house. On the calm, somber, tropical nights, the sound of these falling stones were like sudden thunderclaps. The sleeping younger children, Kenneth, Lynette, Jeanette, and Radhi, would be rudely awakened by these falling stones. They would scream and run to Mangri or Baboo for shelter and comfort. Very often, Baboo would be challenged by the neighborhood men to fight.

Baboo, however, was a quiet, peaceful, and family-oriented person. He would ignore the challenges. This caused the women and men to call him names. Baboo would not respond. He kept on working harder than ever. Frequently, Baboo watched his older children, Frank, Margaret, and Kenneth, being disturbed by the falling stones. Baboo made many complaints at the police precinct, but no arrests were made.

Matters became worse. One dark night in March 1967, a lighted Molotov cocktail was hurled at Baboo's house. The fire ignited the curtains of the windows. Baboo was sewing. When he saw the fire, he became so excited and shocked that he stood up and began moving his hands in all directions, as if he was searching for something in the air.

Frank, who was then sixteen, quickly sprung up on the window ledges and ripped the blazing textiles off their hooks. He threw the fiery curtains through the windows. Again, no one was arrested. The neighbors were so profoundly jealous of Baboo Arjune's progress that they consolidated in their efforts to bring ruin to the Arjune family.

Maybe, when all the odds were down and when one has totally found himself in a corner, that person will grab at the last straw to protect himself or family. Baboo discussed his problems with his African colleagues at the millhouse. His colleagues, in turn, told their friends. One of the friends, an African young man who worked as a chemist in the sugar factory, visited Baboo Arjune's home as a regular customer would.

Junior spoke to Arjune, as his measurements were being taken for a pair of denim pants. He said, "Juggins told me that your neighbors are giving you a hard time. He said that they are stoning your home at nights and have even thrown a Molotov!"

"Man, you are correct, Junior! I am very much disturbed with this situation, and I don't want to get involved. I have many mouths to feed."

"Baboo, you have to do something, man, or these people will walk all over you. These neighbors of yours are what we, Africans, call coolie crabs. Man, like crabs in a bucket, they always try to pull down the one that tries to get to the top!"

Baboo Arjune told Junior to sit down. Baboo took a minute to write down the measurements in his notebook. When he was finished, he said, "You are right in your logic, Junior. I don't mind these people's business. I have problems of my own to think about, man!"

Baboo looked at Junior. He continued talking, "Only yesterday, on my way home from work, that cane-cutter fellow over there threatened to cut me up with his machete. I did not bother the fellow. He walked over to where I was and then threatened me, waving his cutlass."

"I could help you, Baboo. I am a chemist. Of course, you know that! I could make you a few Molotovs that could do great damage to these people. All you have to do is to throw them on all the houses one after the other!"

Baboo became interested. He leaned forward in his chair. He said, "How could I do that, Junior? Man, if I am caught, I will be jailed. All of these people would gang up against me!" Baboo had stretched out his hand in a great arc of a sweep.

"Baboo, you will be foolish to be caught, man. Climb out of southern kitchen window and get to the roof of your house. Walk to the flat of the roof before the elevated V-shaped roof. Remain on that flat roof, the elevation will hide you, and throw the Molotov to the right, left, and center, through the windows of all those who are bothering you."

Mangri was in the kitchen, cooking. Baboo called out to her to fetch him two cups of tea. Frank was in the front verandah, reading. He batted his ears, and his face lightened up. He was interested in the conversation he was overhearing.

Molotov cocktail! Wow! I wish I could make it and stop these vultures in their tracks. I am tired of this stoning! thought Frank. Frank was disturbed during his periods of studying at nights. He was preparing for the London Certificate in Education at the ordinary and Advanced Levels, to be taken in June of 1967. Many nights, he could not concentrate on his work. He would, instead, think of the next stone falling and the repercussions it would cost. He would picture his younger brothers and sisters crying in hysteria, or in his mind's eye, he would see the anguish on his father's face. Frank, at sixteen, was a tall, lanky young man with great agility and stride on his six-foot frame. He was clothed with flesh and sinews that gave him a total weight of 138 pounds, minus his clothes and shoes.

His face was angular, with two big eyes, and he excelled at marathon athletic practices. Frank was training to be a long-distance runner. He loved running as a hobby. This strenuous exercise gave his brown face and body a lean and magnificent look.

Many times Frank had thought of retaliating, but there was always an inner thought that told him to desist. Frank did not want to get the mud from the crab dance. As he reflected, he heard his father asking Junior how he made the Molotov cocktails.

Junior smiled. "Very simple, Baboo! Very simple! Get me the following items and I will make them within two hours. I need one pint of chana [chickpeas), one gallon of gasoline, one pound of pitch, and let's see...how many of these people are bothering you?"

Baboo counted on his fingers, "Seven!" he said.

"Okay, I need ten hundred-watt light bulbs and ten lamp wicks."

"Lord, Junior! What are you going to do with all those things?"

"Very simple, Baboo! When you come home from work tomorrow, soak the chickpeas with gasoline in a large basin. Be careful to put it far away from the fire or light!"

"Junior, I have not decided whether I want to go through with this!" Baboo looked at Junior. He stared at the black face and dark eyes.

"Man, if you want these people to walk on you, if you want them to come in your house and kill all of you, then you will not do what you have to do!"

That did it! Frank breathed a sigh of relief as Baboo spoke, addressing Junior. With a deep sigh, Baboo said, "Okay, Junior, come over tomorrow evening at about 5:00 p.m. The chickpeas will be soaking in a basin in the storeroom below my house. I will have the other stuff waiting."

Mangri brought in the tea. She looked at her husband, then at Junior. She was nonchalant. She returned to her cooking in the kitchen. Baboo offered a cup of tea to Junior. They both sipped their tea.

Baboo said, "I am scared!"

"Aren't we all scared, Baboo? Aren't we? Out of cowardice comes bravery. Ask any hero if he hadn't suffered from fear, doubts, and misgivings!"

"All right, Junior. I will sew your pants free. It is on the house."

Junior drank the last of his tea. He stood up, cup in hand. He walked over, placed his empty teacup on Baboo's machine's cabinet, and stretched out his right hand for a handshake. Baboo shook his hand. "I will see you tomorrow at five, Junior. Goodbye!"

Junior left.

Baboo walked to the kitchen, slowly, contemplating. He told Mangri. Frank joined them. He took his father's hand, saying, "Maybe, Junior is right. We cannot go on like this! Enough is enough!"

Baboo said, "Okay, what will be will be. Let's eat before it gets dark and those bricks start coming again."

That night two more stones were thrown on the roof. Frank went out in the yard, in the dark, to look around. Baboo Arjune and Mangri tried their best to comfort the children. Baboo had no more doubts that something had to be done to stop the neighborhood harassment on his property and his family.

When Baboo was forty-two years old, both his parents died in 1963. His parents were old, very old, and were living in one of the houses owned by Baboo's nephew at Cornelia Ida, on the west coast of Demerara. The old parents were cared for by Baboo's nephew's family, Baboo's niece, and his sister, who lived in close vicinity of Baboo's parents.

At death, it was estimated that Baboo's father was one hundred and five years old and his mother was in her early nineties.

When Baboo's parents had arrived in Guyana, they had no proof of birth in their possessions. They were both indentured. Baboo's father had explained, in Hindi, the only language that he spoke, that one day when he was out in the rice fields in Bengal, India, taking care of his parents' cows as the cattle grazed, he was approached by a group of men who told him of easier jobs of sifting sugar in another state, in India. He was encouraged and influenced by the men to accompany them to a ship so that he could see for himself the kind of sugar he will be given to sift.

In the latter half of the nineteenth century, sugar was a prized commodity in India, and was cultivated by the British in their Indian colony. Baboo's father, in his twenties, decided to accompany the men. The ship was guarded by armed men, but Baboo's father was treated nicely on his way to the ship. It was the last day that Dulamdin ever saw his parents' cattle, his brothers and sisters and parents, and his native India.

When he boarded the ship, he was grabbed and taken to the hold. There he saw many other Indian men, women, and children weeping and being held against their will. Dulamdin became another victim of the indenture system. He was shipped to Guyana, arriving on the British ship, the *Sutlej*, in Port Georgetown in the year 1883.

Baboo's mother, on the other hand, was a young woman when she arrived. In Port Georgetown, the indentured servants were given the ship's papers, stating their names, date of arrival, the ship's name, an assumed age, and the plantation to which they were assigned.

When Baboo's parents died, his father was very tired old man who was literally bent forward with age and the constant laborious work of cleaning the roots of the sugarcane and cutting grass using cutlasses and grass knives.

Mangri's father was also indentured, and he had died in 1955. Baboo grieved for his very old parents and was very sad at their death.

From time to time in his moments of frustration, he would try to think of the frustrations and sadness in the lives of his parents, and he would take comfort from these thoughts. That night, Baboo finally realized that his old parents were gone. He had always known them to be old, and they were gone! He looked at his children and realized that he had a great responsibility to raise his family to be young men and women of intelligence and integrity.

Baboo himself had not done very well at school. He attended classes up to the sixth grade in elementary school. This meager education gave him an insight of the world around him. Baboo had learned to identify with the British culture of the former British colony. He gave all his children English names, and he practiced at home the norms of the pervading British cultural patterns in Guyana.

In the neighborhood in which Baboo lived, in Ocean View Uitvlugt, most of the residents were not interested in sending their children to school beyond the elementary level. Only a few of the neighbors' children in 1967 had ever reached the graduation classes of the elementary schools. The young children were taken out of school and were sent in different directions by their parents. The boys were sent to work in the creole gangs on the sugar plantation--- that is, the parents bought their sons buckets and ropes.

The rope was tied to the handle of the bucket, and on the job as a manure boy at the sugar plantation, the kid would toss the bucket in the manure boy barges that would be anchored in the irrigation canals among the cane fields. The kid pulled on the rope, and as the bucket dragged on the manure, it became filled. The kid then pulled the bucket up on to the dam of the cane field. He lifted the bucket and fetched it to the sugarcane fields. With the bucket in one hand, and rope dangling, the kid bailed the manure with his other hand onto the cane roots. This exercise was repeated over and over again until an eight-hour shift was completed.

In 1967, a kid would work for about fifteen dollars per week as a manure boy. Parents sent their older sons to the cane fields to work as cane harvesters. The matured sugarcanes would first be burnt in the fields. Burning the fields of sugarcanes was done for many reasons. Firstly, by burning, the cane trash was destroyed. This made the cane less hazardous to reap. Secondly, the fires in the fields would scare away or destroy the reptiles, alligators, insects, or carnivores that may have taken refuge there. Thirdly, the mature canes were burnt so as to lessen the water content and to bring the sucrose content of the surface. The third reason was the major reason for sugarcane to burning. It made more economic gains for the sugar planters.

As harvesters, the boys and men manually reaped the sugarcanes. They worked with their cutlasses, chopping the cane about three to six inches above the root. This was done for the purpose of ratooning. The top of the cane or the unburnt trash would also be severed. As the field was reaped, the canes were tied in manageable bundles. The bundles would then be lifted onto the heads of the harvesters, who would fetch them along the beds of the cane fields to the awaiting cane barges.

Harvesting of the sugarcane was the most tedious, strenuous and laborious task of the Guyanese working class people. This difficult task was compounded with working in the hot, tropical climate of the South American mainland.

On the other hand, the teenage girls of Baboo's neighborhood would be taken out of school, before the completion of the elementary level, and would be sent to attend sewing classes. These sewing classes were taught by matronly Guyanese women. The sewing mistresses, as they were called, provided space in their homes to accommodate about a dozen sewing machines at each residence. Each student had to take along her own machine, on which she learnt to sew female and children's clothing.

Sewing was the stepping-stone to marriage. From the time the girl started sewing lessons, the parents would begin looking for a suitable male to wed her. These marriages were mainly arranged, with no love or courtship involved.

Baboo Arjune did not follow the neighborhood norms. At the sugar factory, Baboo observed the white bosses. Baboo also tailored for many of the white bosses. Through his tailoring, he visited the homes of the British overseers, engineers, and managers in the senior staff compound of the sugar estate to take the measurements of the expatriate families. Baboo sewed shorts or summer trunks for the females and khaki and denim outfits for the men and boys of the expatriate families.

During these visits to the senior staff compound, Baboo would pay keen attention to the accommodation and lifestyle of the British. Baboo often wished that he was educated enough to live and dine as the English exhibited. Baboo began to pattern his life and that of his family. He tried to emulate the British as much as was possible.

It was an era in the Guyanese scenario where what was white was right. The country was owned and governed by the British for over three hundred and fifty years. Identification with the British during this time was important for the social and economic advancement of the Guyanese working class. It was important to win the favor of the British for the upward mobility of the Guyanese nationals.

In the educative process, not many of the children of the Guyanese sugar workers or rice farmers were accepted at the two elite schools in Georgetown: Bishop's High School for girls and Queen's College for boys. Only the children of the upper class, the children of the echelon of the society, and the very rich with white learnings were accepted to the top schools of Guyana.

It was an economically structured class society in which Baboo lived in 1967. Baboo worked hard. He labored nights and days to eradicate from his mind the yoke of indentureship to which his forebears were chained. In his thoughts, as he worked among the whites and as he watched their lifestyles, Baboo had relinquished all the bonds of indentureship of his parents. He had freed himself from the degradation of the post bondage of his ancestors, and he had grown determined that his children would have an upbringing and livelihood that would be free from the ties of the land. Baboo bore no hate, no grudge, or no enmity for his parents' misfortune. He felt that their indentureship was their fate, but he was living in a society in which one had to strive for economic stability. Baboo realized that education would play the major role in the future development of his country. He knew that the British would soon have to leave his young and recently independent country and that Guyanese would have to face the future on their own.

Baboo knew that Guyanese would have to be educated, through which they would be capable to make the transition from colonial dominance to a Guyanese takeover of the means of production, the infrastructure, and the government.

Baboo, therefore, thought of educating his children and turning his back on the estate norm of his village. As he personally strove for betterment, he was hated by his own people. It was with disgust in his mind, after the last two stones had fallen, that he fully accepted Junior's proposal.

On his way home from work the following day, Baboo made his purchases. He soaked the chickpeas in the gasoline and awaited Junior's arrival. Junior came at about 6:00 p... He went in at the front of Baboo's house, in view of the inquisitive eyes. Baboo took him through the house and down the rear staircase to the storeroom below the elevated stilted house. Junior, with a large pair of electrical pliers, carefully unscrewed the stem of the lightbulbs.

"Why are you taking off the head of the bulbs?" Baboo asked.

"Be quiet, man. We do not want those neighbors to hear. Watch, and you will see exactly what I am doing." Junior worked deftly as he spoke.

He laid the "decapitated" bulbs side by side on the workbench. Junior looked at Baboo.

He said, "Fetch me a few pieces of wood, any size between four inches to a foot long, that I can use to prop up those bulbs as I fill them with the soaked chickpeas and gasoline."

Baboo hurriedly got Junior's request. One by one, using a tablespoon and a cup, Junior filled each light bulb with gasoline and the very much swollen chickpeas. As he finished one, he propped it up on the work bench with pieces of wood. Baboo caught on to what Junior was doing. He went in search of more scrap wood.

"Do you have a little basket with a handle, Baboo?" asked Junior.

"I think I do," replied Baboo.

"Good, man, great! Get it down here."

Baboo left and shortly returned with the basket. It was capable of storing about two dozen eggs. Baboo set it down on the workbench. Junior inserted a kerosene lamp wick into each of the bulb, allowing the greater part of the wick to soak into the gasoline. He left about an inch to protrude above the opening of the bulb.

Baboo watched with interest. Junior then sealed the remaining opening at the neck of the bulb with the semi-soft pitch. Having completed this, he laid the loaded bulbs, delicately handling them, one at a time, in the basket. Between every two bulbs, Junior stuck a used piece of old cotton cloth.

He looked at Baboo when he was finished. He spoke to no one in particular, addressing the filled basket, "That's a damn beautiful deadly arsenal that can cause one hell of a confusion." He smiled. He patted Baboo on the shoulder. He said, "Baboo, I know that you are worried. I do know that you do not mean to harm these people around you. But at the same time, you want peace. But, man, some- times you have to fight with fire to make peace! Let's say you give them a final chance, and if they stone your house tonight, you then Molotov cocktail them in return, man."

"That's the part I am worried about, Junior. I do not have the mind to be that angry. I do not think I will be able to throw those things, Junior," Baboo solemnly replied.

"Look here, Baboo! You are a very good friend of my African brothers. The boys say that you treat them nicely in the factory. Because of your kindness to my brothers, I will return a favor to you tonight. Go get us some beers, man, and you and I will cut some time here tonight. I don't have to work until 2:00 p.m. tomorrow!" Junior looked at Baboo with a challenge in his eyes. Baboo turned and peered through the door of his storeroom. The six o'clock bees were droning in the trees. The fiery sun was sinking beyond the crimsoned and blotched skyline, and twilight was spreading its wings across the land.

Baboo said quietly, with mischief twinkling in his brown eyes, his gold teeth shimmering in the light of the bulb as he smiled between words, "Not very often am I offered a favor, Junior. Not very often! I take your offer. Remain here, man. I don't want you to step out or the neighbors will see you. Probably by now they may feel that you have left. Also, they will be convinced that I harbor no strangers if I should step out alone to get us the beers. I will ride my bicycle, as if all is normal!" Baboo, in a friendly gesture, slapped Junior on the shoulder. Junior returned the friendly slap.

"Baboo, I like you, man. If they bother you tonight, we are going to make them do the shindig, man. Yes, we will make them dance!"

As Baboo turned to leave, Frank rapped on the door. Junior became instantly alert. Baboo cracked the door and peered out. He saw Frank. He quickly let Frank in. Frank looked around and instantly understood. Baboo opened his mouth to speak, but Frank motioned him to be quiet. Baboo then told Frank to keep Junior's company while he went to the grocery store. Frank smiled to his father, who left without further hesitation. He went upstairs and told Mangri what had been decided. Mangri was skeptical.

"Be very careful, man. I am very frightened," she said.

"Don't be worried. Close the windows and give the children to eat. After dinner, you and the children should go to bed. Later, if there are any stones, try to calm the children and keep them in their rooms. Frank will be with us downstairs." Baboo held Mangri's hand in his and gave them a pacifying squeeze. He left her standing in the kitchen, looking at his tall figure as he walked through the house. Baboo was still clad in his greasy working clothes with his stained white fiberglass helmet on his head. He stepped down the front stairs, took up his bicycle, and cycled to the grocery shop.

In the meantime, in the storeroom, Frank moved closer to the workbench and looked at the basket of Molotov bombs. He touched one.

Junior said, "Wash your hand with soap, Frank. I do not want you to smell of gasoline. While your father is gone, I will clean up here and remove all traces of gasoline and the other materials we have used." Junior collected all the remains and placed them in the basin. He asked Frank, "How could I get to your pit latrine? I want to dispose of this stuff." Frank pointed the way.

By this time darkness had quickly fallen on the village. Junior quickly and stealthily made his way to the disposal site. When he returned, he washed the basin and the workbench with liquid soap mixed with Smell-o-Pine. The storeroom scented with the freshness of the pine liquid. Junior then settled down on a chair, stretching out his long legs.

He looked at Frank and said, "I heard that you are studying for your examinations. What job would you like to do when you leave school, young man?"

"I will write my examinations in June, and if I pass, I will apply to be a teacher," replied Frank.

"I don't like that 'if.' Try to be more positive! You should say, "When I pass," Junior admonished in his friendly voice.

"Okay. When I pass, I will apply to teach, as from September," said Frank.

"Attaboy! I am happy for you! Education is the gateway to life. The entire world is a university, and education opens your eyes to the workings of this universe of ours." Junior's eyes twinkled. He was warming up to his subject. As a chemist, Junior read widely. He could speak on almost any topic, as any educated Guyanese would do.

"The door to knowledge is through education. Learning, as the proverb goes, is better than silver and gold. Not many of you Indian children go far to school, boy! I think that you people have to try. You have to take a page out of the book of the African Guyanese. They believe in education, boy! As you may have observed, most of the teachers, nurses, and public servants in this country are presently African Guyanese!" Junior was proud of his people. He looked at Frank, expecting a reply. Junior loved to indulge in conversations on education and learning.

Frank retorted, "I agree with you. That is why these people hate us. I am attending high school in Georgetown, and my other brothers and sisters are all going to school. None of us have begun to work on the sugar plantation, like most of the other children around here. Added to that, my father is a very progressive man. He is a hard worker, and he does not find the time to indulge in idle gossips with the neighbors." Frank took a deep breath. It was a long speech, and he did not very often have the opportunity to talk to strangers. On the other hand, Frank was a very good speaker. He was a member of the debating society at his alma mater.

"Your father will be proud if he hears you talk, Frank. My friends told me that Baboo usually boast to them about his educational plans for his children. You have a good father, boy, and he loves his children. We, the Africans, do not like to see people take advantage on kind and ambitious men." Junior stretched out his hand and patted Frank on the shoulder. "Try to take your education, boy. This country needs educated people. Who will take over from the white people when they leave? You think of that, boy, and study hard! Kindly have me excused, I want to take a smoke." Junior reached into his shirt pocket and took out his Bristol cigarettes and his lighter.

Frank turned to leave. Junior quickly said, "No! No! Don't leave. I do not mean for you to go. I only want to have a smoke." Junior extracted a cigarette and tapped the butt on the lighter, making the tobacco within more compact. He lit up. Frank lashed out with his right hand at the pesky mosquitoes that had started to bite already. "They are persistent pests around here."

"Parasites, Frank! Parasites! We have to live with them. Too much stagnant water around. No proper drainage in these sugar villages," Junior contributed.

At that moment, Baboo rapped on the door. Frank peered out and let his father in. Frank then left and shortly after returned with a lighted mosquito destroyer. It was an incensed clay coil, manufactured with mosquito repellants. It kept the flying parasites away from their sources of nurture.

Baboo placed a dozen beers, ice, a can of corned mutton, and crackers on the workbench. He sent Frank to fetch him glasses and a plate with onions and peppers for the corned mutton. Frank left. Darkness had pervaded outside. There were no streetlamps. The village was dismal and humid. People were indoors, extricating themselves from the annoyance of the mosquitoes and the heat of the streaming streets.

Baboo moved over to a bent nail embedded in the wall, and he used it to snap off the corks of two Bank beers. He passed a beer to Junior. Frank returned with the glasses, filled with ice, and passed one each to the men. They poured and drank to each other. Frank opened the canned corned mutton and poured it onto the plate with the sliced inions and peppers. He used a spoon to mix the contents of the plate thoroughly. Frank then opened a can of Pepsi Cola and made himself a biscuit sandwich. The men drank and helped themselves to sandwiches.

Junior said, "Baboo, it is dark outside, and it's nearly 7:30 p.m. At about what time do those creatures out there start their bombardment?"

At about 8:00 p.m., or from then on," replied Baboo.

"I want you to switch the light off. If you have a storm lantern, light it and place it in the corner. I want as little light as possible. After our second beer, we will go and keep watch in the dark. I want to see the directions from which the stones are thrown." Junior drank deeply into his Banks.

The night became pitch dark. It was moonless. The stars twinkled far away in the distant sky. Bats jollied themselves in their habitat, and owls screeched from the roof tops. It was a glorifying night for the devil's play. Baboo and Junior stepped out from the storeroom. Frank tiptoed behind them. The mosquitoes zoomed in on their preys. The men and boy stood in the dark behind the concrete stilts of the house. They waited until their eyes became adjusted to the darkness.

They were there only for about eight minutes, listening in the eerie silence of the tropical gloom, when the night's calmness was shattered by a nerve-racking blast---*baddam* ---the sound of heavy stone hitting the galvanized sheet with a force. Upon contact with the roof, the stone rolled away with its momentum, until it fell over the edge with a thump on the concrete sidewalk in the yard.

Junior whispered, "Baboo, that one came from the east. The stone rolled and fell off from the western roof."

"You are right. That's the bastard who threatened me," Baboo replied, much agitated.

Bam! Bam! Two more stones struck and fell. One crashed down on the southern sidewalk and one on the eastern side of the house. *Crash!* Shattered glass and shards fell on the concrete below, on the northern side of the house, which was below the front verandah. As they listened, they heard the stone rolling in the house.

"My God! I hope that my children are not injured," Baboo said frantically. Junior rushed over to Baboo. "Be quiet, man. The children are not screaming. Your wife didn't shout. They are safe so far. Remain there and listen."

Baboo calmed down. Frank quietly tiptoed upstairs to see if all was well. He shortly returned and reported that the children were crying, but that his mother had them under control in her bedroom.

Junior touched Baboo's hand. "Let's return quietly to the storeroom. I have heard and seen enough!" No more stones were thrown.

"Go upstairs to your verandah and make a shout that they have broken your glass windows. Remain upstairs and let yourself be seen. Leave the rear door open when you have entered the house." Junior gave Baboo an assuring shove. Junior looked at Frank. He said, "You better go also. Stand with your father, so that you will not be implicated in whatever may happen." Junior stretched out his right hand to Frank. Frank shook Junior's hand. "Good luck, kid," Junior said.

"Good luck, Junior," replied Frank.

Frank was angry. He was tempted to grab a few stones and to throw them to left, right, and center. He wanted to destroy his tormentors. He wanted to see them dead. The adrenaline boiled in his veins until his face was suffused with anger. However, Frank quietly walked up the back stairs and stood by his father when Baboo shouted that they had broken his window. Baboo screamed that he will report this attack to the police and that he knew who were destroying his house and tormenting his family. Baboo called Mangri to get the broom and the dustpan.

Mangri did as was requested. She swept and picked up the shards from the polished floor. She pierced her finger in the process. Baboo grabbed a walking stick and stood in his front verandah. He paced to and fro.

About half an hour later, when all was calm and quiet and the tropical night sounds had once again pervaded the atmosphere, there was another crash, much lighter this time, and the broken windowpane on the opposite house was heard crashing to the ground. Then the curtain of the neighbor's house caught fire. Loud screams were heard from next door. Many tiny fires had started, and they were engulfing the carpet of the house.

More screams were heard ---they came from the east and the west, they came from the northern houses opposite. Many fires had started on every premises as the windows shattered and as the statured chickpeas rolled in balls of fire, igniting whatever were in their path.

The night's solemnity was rudely broken all around. There were repeated shouts of "Fire! Fire! Help! Help!" Curtains, covering sheets of chairs, door blinds, and carpets were all ablaze in all the houses around Baboo's. People ran in all directions and scrambled for buckets, forming bucket brigades, fighting the fires with water taken from storage drums in the various yards.

Pandemonium had broken loose. There were no fire engines in the vicinity. People, in crowds from the village, ran from one blazing house to the other, dousing the blazing fires with hundreds of buckets of water. There was panting, grunting, moaning, and screaming!

Baboo and Frank also ran out with their buckets. They also helped to douse the fires with buckets of water. They also mingled with the crowds, laboring and breathing heavily as they filled their buckets, ran upstairs, and splashed their fires. Their enemies saw them helping. Recognition dawned, consciences were questioned, but words were not spoken. The battle waged on. Gradually the blazes ebbed and were eventually relinquished. The fires did not last very long. The army of water throwers were victorious over the chickpeas. The houses were, however, badly scorched. Textiles were seared and damaged beyond further use. Much expense was incurred, as the melee subsided within the hour.

Baboo and Frank went home, tired and frightened. Junior had left. He had vanished in the night, and the remaining beers had also vanished. Baboo smiled at the realization. He made a mental note to thank Junior the following day.

Baboo did not know what the repercussions may be with his neighbors in the future. He was extremely happy that none of the houses were made uninhabitable. Occupation could have resumed in the houses after a few hours of cleaning and tidying. Baboo, as if to wash the guilt from his mind, told Frank and Mangri that much before he retired to bed that night.

Baboo's family slept fitfully that night. Their sleep was frequented with dreams of commotions and fear of being hunted. Baboo dreamt that he was swimming in the ocean toward his family, who were drowning. Every time he stretched out his hand to rescue one of his children, the child went under, and Baboo became frenzied and frantic. Baboo awoke with a start when Mangri was slipping away from his grasp. Baboo was sweating profusely as he sat in bed and looked around.

All seemed well. His family was sleeping. All human noises had ceased outside, and he could only have distinguished the regular night sounds. In his backyard, one of his cocks crowed, then another, then it spread around the neighborhood, cocks flapping their wings and crowing everywhere.

As Baboo wiped the sweat from his body, he looked at the clock on the night table. It was 4:00 a.m., the usual time for the cocks to crow. Baboo listened, and he heard pots and pans rattling, clanging, falling. He heard water spurting through several artesian standpipes in the yards. Baboo breathed a sigh of relief. They had lived through the night. He was listening to the usual morning sounds of the wives and mothers of the estate's back dam workers, who had arisen as usual to prepare breakfast and lunch for their husbands and sons to take to their workplaces in the fields aback of the sugar factory.

The field workers would leave their homes at about 5:00 a.m. to catch the labor punts/barges that would transport them for many miles aback of the sugar factories to the cane fields to harvest, to chop and plant (cultivate), to clean the cane roots, or to spray and manure the sugarcane (pest control).

Baboo felt remorse, as he thought of his neighbors and their day's toil in the blistering sunshine of the natural scenic backlands. Why, he wondered, would these hardworking people, who daily sweat, pant, and fatigue for a livelihood envy their own kind who were trying to elevate themselves from the dullness of the society? Why, he wondered, did these people content themselves to be in academic decadence when he knew that they could strive for a brighter future with political independence of the country?

Baboo knew that sooner or later, the emphasis in the society would be upon education, and that the working-class people of the rural areas would soon make a drastic turnaround. He knew, by passing through the other villages, that almost every home was making a desperate effort to at least send one child to high school and beyond. He knew of many families who had been making tremendous sacrifices to keep one or two children in school uniforms with book bags.

Why couldn't the eyes of his neighbors be opened to the light of change? Baboo prayed, that his neighbors should live and learn. He wished them well. He hoped and prayed that they would leave him and his family to live in peace and prosperity as they strived to gain and to build their future. He hoped that his neighbors would be reawakened soon and that they would not live to perish in their morbid insanity.

The days went by, and nothing happened. The stoning had ceased. As his neighbors passed Baboo, they saluted him or greeted him with respect. "Good morning" or "good afternoon" never ceased to pass their lips in salutation.

At first, Baboo was surprised, then he gradually accepted the change in behavior. He was shocked when the male neighbors came over and asked him to sew their clothes. Baboo never refused them. Instead, he tried to be as neat as possible with his new customers' clothing. Old enmities were gradually forgotten, matters were mended, and life progressed smoothly in the vicinity of Baboo's residence.

Frank and the other children continued their schooling. On the first day of May 1967, Radhi was six years old. On that day he started out at kindergarten. Margaret, Kenneth, Lynette, and Jeanette were all doing well in elementary school. Mangri continued helping with the hemming and the buttons, and to take care of her family.

One day, Mangri asked, "Baboo, why are you killing yourself with all this work? Why don't you take a rest, man?"

Baboo replied, "Rest is for the lazy! I will rest when I am dead."

"Don't be stupid, man. Don't speak like that--you can't die and leave this houseful of children on me alone!" Mangri admonished.

"That is why I am working so many hours! I want to have enough money in the bank, so that if I die, you will be able to take care of the children. We have a big house here. There are no debts owed on this house, so now we can't go wrong if we should have our own money."

Mangri did not reply. She felt that her husband knew best. Of course, she reasoned, he was the breadwinner!

Chapter

2

When Baboo strove for peace with his neighbors, he was also plagued with problems from the marriage from his second daughter, Lena. The marriages of Baboo's two elder daughters were additional reasons why the neighbors had hated the family of Baboo Arjune.

Mona, the eldest daughter, was married to Hanoman Singh, who was a station master with the Transport and Harbors Department. Hanoman Singh was an educated and intelligent young man who had worked his way up from clerk to station master in a very short time through competition, diligence, and grim determination.

When Mona had grown into a beautiful young woman, many of the village boys had sought her hand in marriage, but Baboo had refused the offers. Baboo did not want Mona to be married to a sugar estate back dam worker. He had felt that that would not have been a glorious future for her.

Baboo's refusal of the marriage offers for Mona had flashed around the village like wildfire. The neighbors had felt Baboo had despised his own people, that Baboo had scorned his own people. They discussed Baboo wherever they had gathered. They agreed among themselves that Baboo was professing to be a white man and to live like the whites. They were not tolerant of Baboo's rejection of their village youths, of their own sons.

On the other hand, Baboo, who was much enlightened, felt that Mona should have a choice in her marriage. He did not believe in the village norm to send Mona to sewing and then marry her off to the first suitor that passed by.

When Mona got married to Hanoman, that marriage broke the village tradition of a plantation girl being wedded to a plantation boy. It was the beginning of change that made the villagers envious. However, this marriage was inevitable. Hanoman had hailed from Bartica, in the upper Essequibo, which was over a hundred miles from Baboo's residence, and not from the plantation system.

When Hanoman and Mona first met in 1963, it was love at first sight. The marriage worked well, and by 1967, three children, two boys and a girl, were born to this happily married couple. They grew and prospered in marriage.

On the other hand, Baboo's second daughter's marriage was packed with brutality and intrigues. However, the neighbors were not aware of the animosity, hatred, and disastrous nature of this marriage. All they knew was that Baboo Arjune's second daughter was married to a teacher, and they seethed with envy. They felt that Baboo was indeed "high class."

Baboo thanked Junior. Junior had opened their eyes to their own wrongdoing. Baboo now had to contend with Lena's problems. He had felt that indeed there was no rest for his tired body. Why, he reasoned, are there so many problems in this life?

The highlight of Baboo's life was when Frank was successful at his examination. Baboo boasted, in friendly chatter to his workmates that his son had done well and that he had applied for the position of student teacher. Apart from the tedious work to earn cash, Baboo had tried in many other ways to make his family comfortable.

One of the problems of the villagers was to get their daily supply of potable water. The water was obtained from an artesian standpipe located on the village road in close proximity to the house around Baboo's. The society had not reached the stage of development in the early sixties to facilitate potable water in the homes of the rural villages. As a result, villagers had to collect their water supply from communal artesian pipes.

Villagers were often greedy and spiteful pertaining to this essential routine. They frequently took dozens of buckets to the water fountain because it was the unwritten rule among them that water was collected on a first come, first served basis. Anyone who was in an emergency to collect a bucket of water would have to wait in the blistering sunshine of hours, sometimes before her bucket would be filled, on her turn. If a person was disliked, that person would have to wait an eternity, because spiteful villagers would sometimes line up not only with buckets but also five-and ten-gallon drums.

To worsen the situation, and to make waiting for one's turn a greater annoyance, was that the artesian "fountain" did not give off water with great pressure. The communal pipes were also the meeting place for neighborhood gossiping. It was the grapevine from which all news were transmitted via the human wavelengths. It was also the venue where many women's disputes were settled, either verbally or "fistfully."

Baboo did not want his family to be involved in the neighborhood water melee. For Baboo, time was precious; time meant, for him, work and money. He needed his wife to help him in is manufacturing enterprise rather than wasting valuable hours to get water.

To be independent of the village standpipes, in the early sixties, Baboo had bought a huge condemned steam boiler from the sugar factory. It was a long cylindrical boiler, thirty-five feet in length by six feet in diameter. The cylindrical iron sheeting that composed the boiler was one inch in thickness.

The day Baboo brought the boiler home was like a picnic in the village. Almost everyone turned out, men, women and children, to give their advice, or to lend a helping hand, or to watch as the boiler was dragged across the public road, then unto the village road, sliding its way on ramps.

First, Baboo got the boiler loaded onto a huge barge that was used to transport heavy-duty machineries to the cane fields for plowing purposes. The boiler was loaded onto the barge by the crane hoist at the waterfront of the sugar factory. Baboo had help that day from about one hundred of his fellow factory workers who were off duty.

It was a Sunday morning, and the factory was shut down for the day, being the rest day. Huge chains were strapped around the boiler at the two ends and at the middle, for equilibrium and for safety hoisting. In the barge, the boiler was set down on inward-sloping greenheart piles, twelve by twelve inches in dimensions.

Baboo and his African charge hands directed the transportation of the boiler. A huge, high-powered bulldozer was used to pull the loaded, weighted-down barge along the main irrigation canal to Baboo's village. At the village, the boiler, after many chains had snapped, was taken out from the barge and dragged by the bulldozer, foot by foot sliding on greenheart ramps to Baboo's home. Baboo had to break down his front fence to let the boiler be taken through his yard to reach his backyard, where it was set up close to the rear end of his house. Once the boiler was in place, Baboo entertained his friends.

Mangri, along with many of the village women, had prepared over one hundred pounds of curried mutton, fifty pounds of dhal puri (a delicacy made from wheaten flour and yellow split peas), eight gallons of parboiled rice, and a huge pot of split pea soup. For liquid refreshments, Baboo supplied several gallons of El Dorado Bonded Reserve Rum and crates of Pepsi Cola.

Before the entertainment started, Chester, Baboo's charge hand, moved a toast. He said, "Gentlemen, to our success in bringing home this huge steam boiler, and may Baboo have fresh steam for the rest of his life!"

Carroll echoed, "Cheers to our good supervisor, Baboo, and may he and his family drink cool water forever!"

Everyone cheered and laughed. They drank deeply of the iced El Dorado Rum laced with Pepsi. After the last drink was taken, Baboo shouted, "Gentlemen, let's pour again!" They took their refill and looked at Baboo. In their eyes, they showed their love for this gentleman with whom they worked.

Baboo said above the din of their voices, "Gentlemen, I am very grateful for your help today. On behalf of my family and I, and my neighbors also, because they may also drink from that boiler"---the crowd cheered ---"I wish to thank you from the bottom of my heart.

I will not dare to repay you for this great help, but I will forever be in your debt. Gentlemen, eat and drink and let's be merry. Thank you, and cheers!" They drank. They clapped their hands. They were tired but happy.

Mangri and the ladies set huge basins of food upon the makeshift tables. They stacked plates, forks, and spoons. Huge buckets of iced water were also set up. Manu of the neighbors had joined in. Baboo had welcomed them. They ate, they drank. After a few drinks, they sang. They rhymed their own songs, made their own music with spoons, plates, empty bottles, and drummed on the tabletops. They created their usual Guyanese percussion band. It was a great group of merry men who dined at Baboo's home that Sunday. Most of them had visited his home before, had drunk with him, but that Sunday, they shared a special bond of camaraderie.

As the days went by, Baboo brought home his tools---wrenches, sledgehammers, and heavy-duty jacks. Baboo worked alone, with Frank positioning the boiler, east to west, and casting a concrete foundation around it. It was tedious, back-breaking work, but Baboo persisted, suspending his tailoring and putting in all available time at his disposal.

When the boiler was solidly laid in the desired place, Baboo embarked on sandblasting both the inside and exterior. No electrical-powered or automatic-powered machinery was available at that time in Baboo's locality. The sandblasting was therefore done with brutal strength and manpower, using the sledgehammer and engineering hammers and cold chisels. As Baboo pounded the thick corroded iron boiler, Frank used a long-handled steel bristled brush to brush away the remnants of the corrosion.

Working in the interior of the boiler was stifling and very uncomfortable. The boiler was a complete cylindrical casting, with both ends of the cylinder soundly attached and sealed in the middle of the base. At one end of the boiler was a manhole that was insufficient to let enough light or air into the interior of the boiler. Working inside was therefore suffocating and painstaking. Baboo and Frank worked with lanterns and torchlights. The lanterns made breathing more difficult. It fed upon the limited oxygen supply within. Added to all this discomfiture was the excessive heat given off and encompassing within the boiler, owing to the tropical sun directing its rays upon the steel structure in an atmospheric temperature that was almost constant at 98 degrees Fahrenheit.

Baboo never gave up until the interior of the boiler was completely cleaned and tarred. After tarring the boiler, Baboo left the manhole open for a week until he was certain that the heat had thoroughly dried the tar. Then he used wrenches to refit the sealings of the aperture. At the bottom of the boiler, Baboo had drilled a hole from which he attached a length of three quarters of an inch cylindrical galvanized pipe. At the end of the pipe, away from the boiler, Baboo attached a faucet.

As Baboo worked, his neighbors watched in awe. A few came over to offer their help sometimes. Most times they would stand and watch as Baboo worked. They both admired and hated him. How could one man accomplished so much in so short time? They frequently asked themselves. A time or two, they asked Baboo why he worked so hard. He would reply, "Time was limited."

As Baboo worked, he thought of his second daughter, Lena. Why was she suffering? Why was her husband, the young man who claimed he loved her, who defied his parents and demanded to marry her when she was only fourteen years old, now ill-treating her?

Baboo loved his children. Baboo loved Lena. He had received many complaints from Lena's neighbors that Lena was often brutalized by her husband and her in-laws. Baboo heard the complaints and took no action. Maybe, he pacified himself, the complaints were only false allegations. Maybe they were the tales of the rumor mongers! Baboo was uneasy. He plunged himself into almost continuous work to take his mind off Lena. Baboo comforted himself with the thought that Lena was living at her in-laws and that all was well and good with her.

Baboo continued working on his boiler. He enjoyed and appreciated his skill and dexterity. At the eastern end, on the upper surface of the boiler, Baboo used an oxyacetylene torch to cut a hole large enough for him to insert a cone-shaped funnel with metal sieve within the cone. The diameter of the upper end of the funnel was twelve inches. Baboo attached a long cylindrical aluminum pipe, three inches in diameter, from the gutter of the roof of his house to the funnel on the boiler. As he progressed on the job, more and more neighbors and friends gathered to watch him work. They admired his engineering feat. They commented, criticized, and offered their advice, but Baboo was heedless. He merely chatted with them and worked on.

As Baboo completed his job on the boiler, the May-June rains came. Within two weeks, the boiler was filled. The water spilled over from the opening at the funnel. Baboo reopened the bottom of the boiler and let the water steadily empty itself. He let thousands of gallons of water flow into his yard. As he let the water out, his yard was flooded, but within minutes the water receded into the village drainage outlets.

When Baboo was certain that there were no more oils remaining in the boiler, he reinstalled and resealed his three-quarter-inch cylindrical pipe at the bottom. Quickly the boiler was refilled. The communal well was thought of no more. Baboo and his family now had a readily available supply of water for drinking, cooking, and bathing purposes.

As the weeks progressed, Baboo realized that his family had to withdraw the water from the boiler in the yard and fetch the buckets up the many flights of stairs into the kitchen. Sometimes Baboo noticed the younger children spilling the water on the stairs as they climbed. This made the stairs very slippery and dangerous. A few times Baboo noticed the children would stumble with their weighted buckets, and they went tumbling down the stairs. He felt that the children may one day seriously injure themselves if he did not do something to rectify the situation.

Baboo thought of a plan. At the factory, he had seen many discarded metal pipes of various lengths and of various cylindrical diameters. He spoke to his factory manager and asked whether he could purchase a few lengths of the cast-iron, four-inches diametered, cylindrical pipes. Baboo explained his plan to his boss. Instead of charging him for the materials, Baboo was given permission to select what materials he required and to go ahead with his construction, providing that he used his own time to do his private work.

Baboo constructed a huge four-posted iron frame, rectangular in shape. The base of the rectangle was six feet by eight. The frame was erected to allow five feet of length to be cemented, as the foundation, in the earth; twenty-five feet was to rise above the ground and higher than the roof of Baboo's kitchen. At the top of the upright rectangular frame, Baboo used two cast-iron pipes to build a platform, four feet by twelve feet. On the platform, Baboo welded four fifty-five-gallon steel drums. At the top of the drums were welded covers, with spouts for an overflow.

At the factory Baboo was helped by his friends in the construction of the iron frame. This structure became known as overhead tanks. After Baboo had installed the overhead tanks on the western end of the boiler, Baboo drilled another hole in his boiler and attached a hand pump with cut-off valves. With three-quarter-inch pipelines, the hand pump was attached to the overhead tanks. Through the pipelines, Baboo led the water from the overhead tank to sinks that he installed in his kitchen and his living room.

Many of neighbors and villagers had come to admire Baboo's latest construction. As he installed these engineering devices, Baboo and his family also earned the envy of many. But he was heedless of criticism. He believed in "a time to be born and a time to live and work." Manually, Baboo and the children worked on the handpump to fill the overhead tanks. Because of its height, when the taps were turned on in the kitchen or the living room, the water spurted with extreme pressure.

Mangri and the children were now very happy. Gone were the days when they had to fetch water up the stairs. Long past were the days when they had to go to the village artesian well to get water. The family was now more private to pursue their lives, and there was less cause now to unnecessarily mingle with the villagers.

Baboo's ultimate aim was to live in peace and privacy. It is a marvel to think of the many things a Guyanese is capable of doing. With limited tools and equipment, with lack of an adequate education, most

Guyanese men are capable of being jacks of many trades. Although they may not be masters of many, Guyanese try to help themselves as much as possible. They are very hardworking and complex people.

Lena was at elementary school, popularly called the primary school, and she was in the sixth standard, which is equivalent to the eighth grade, when Cholan Nauth joined the faculty of the school. Cholan was a young teacher, twenty years of age, who had been successful at the London General Certificate in Education. His success at this examination gained him access to the teaching profession.

Cholan was a young man who spoke with clenched teeth. He was five feet eight inches tall, with a brown complexion. His face was angular, with a deep incline on his cheek. He had a straight nose that was flat between the dark brown eyes, and his lips were slightly protruded. His hair was black, greased, and combed backward. His face was pockmarked and bare. He was of medium built and weighed about one hundred and forty-five pounds.

As a new teacher, Cholan assisted in teaching the eighth grade class, which was Lena's. As he moved around the class on his first day, he saw a lanky beauty who sat in the front seat. He was attracted to her presence because of the peculiar way in which she wrote. She was left-handed, and she wrote with her notebook lying sideways on the desk.

At fourteen, Lena was five feet seven inches tall and slim of waist and ankles. She had waist-long hair that was well groomed and spread on her shoulders and back. As she smiled, her beautiful face dimpled, and her brown eyes danced in merriment. Lena, in all likeness, was a light brown, slim, East Indian beauty, and she was bright. She became more noticeable to Cholan, because she would finish her work very quickly and stand to get them checked. When the class did mental arithmetic, Lena would frequently raise her hand to solve the mental mathematics. When the class was tested in spelling or dictation, Lena would frequently spell her words or correctly write the passage that was dictated. She was the girl that was bright! She caught the eyes of Cholan.

During his second week on the job, without the consent of the teacher, Cholan asked Lena to see him after school. Lena was frightened, but she remained as requested. The headmaster was also in school, giving extra lessons to his scholarship class. When Cholan had sat at his desk, he asked Lena to sit on a bench opposite him. School had dismissed at 3:00 p.m. The students had left. Most of the teachers had already gone. It was about 3:15 p.m.

He said to her, "Lena, I think that you are a brilliant student. If continue to do as well as you do, you could be successful at the graduation examinations, and maybe you could be appointed here as a pupil teacher."

Lena felt flattered. She blushed, brushing away the hair from her eyes. She replied, "Mr. Nauth, I am trying to do my best. I would like to pass my examinations and to be a teacher. Mr. Horton, my class teacher, told me that he will help me to get a position here if I am successful at the examination." She looked at him. His brown eyes were staring at her as she spoke.

He smiled and said, "That is the way to think. Keep on working,"

Lena said, "Thank you, Mr. Nauth. Is that what you wanted to see me about? I have to go now. My mother would be worried if I am late."

"Remain a few minutes more and I will help you with your math. With what topic do you think you need the most help?"

Lena thought for a while. She was afraid. She said, "I have to go. All my friends have left. Maybe I will discuss it with mother and let her know what you have said. I will let you know tomorrow if I can remain after school."

"Okay, let us go. Maybe I can accompany you if you are walking home," said Cholan.

"That would not be nice! What would the people say? I am afraid that my mother will know that you have followed me home!" Lena was terrified.

"Don't be afraid. I will walk along with you," insisted Cholan.

They left the school premises together. Lena lived about three quarters of a mile from the school. It was customary for her to walk to and from school in the mornings and evenings in the company of her classmates and her siblings. That evening, Mangri was worried when the other children arrived home and Lena did not. Mangri asked the older children, Frank and Margaret, if they had seen Lena. Both the children replied that they had waited five minutes after school in the appointed meeting place for Lena, but she did not show up. They said they decided to walk home without her.

Mangri reprimanded the children, "Do you know that is dangerous for you children to cross the streets by yourselves? Those streets are very busy! Anything could have happened!"

"Ma, we were very careful. We crossed with the school's safety patrol. All went well. We also walked along with the crowd," Frank replied.

"That's not the point. Where is Lena? She was supposed to accompany you children!" Mangri paced nervously, whispering under her breath, "That girl is supposed to be here by now! She did not tell me that she would be late. I have to let Baboo know about this."

As Cholan and Lena walked, he told her about himself and family. He said that his father was a Pandit (Hindu priest) and businessman, and that his father owned a large textile store and Uitvlugt Front. He said that he had five brothers and six sisters.

As Lena walked along, she became less bashful and scared. She expressed her surprise. She said, "That is a very big family! We are five sisters and three brothers. My elder sister is already married, and still there seems to be so many of us at home! How do you guys get along?"

"We get along well. There are often quarrels and fights among us, but the bigger ones always step in to make peace. There are no major problems. Two of us brothers are now working. The other children are going to school. We all help each other."

"All my other brothers and sisters also go to school. My mother is a housewife. My father works at the sugar factory and does tailoring part time."

I do not know your parents, but from what you have said, it seems as if your dad is doing well," replied Cholan.

"We are doing well, and my father is a very hard worker," Lena retorted.

"My parents are very busy in the store. A few of my brothers and sisters help them sometimes. But let's talk about you -- do you like school? Do you have friends?"

"Yes, I love school, and I hope to go on to college someday. I want to get very qualified, to get a good job and be able to help my parents and my brothers and sisters," Lena replied.

"Well, I don't want to help my parents. They are very rich. I want to help myself by working and attending the university. To accomplish this, I will have to travel to Georgetown to attend classes in the evenings. It will be very difficult. Travelling will take up lots of time," Cholan said.

"I learned about the university by reading the newspapers. My father also said that it was established by the PPP government recently, in 1962, and that it is housed at Queen's College in Georgetown," Lena had replied.

"Your father is correct," said Cholan, "The campus for the University of Guyana is now under construction at Turkeyen. In the meantime, classes have started at QC. I intend to apply to do my Bachelor of Arts degree and to major in Spanish." Cholan spoke with pride and confidence.

Lena looked at him. She was happy for him. She felt that Cholan was very ambitious and that he would probably have a very bright future. She asked, "Who is the principal of the university? Is he a Guyanese?"

Cholan quickly answered her, "No, he is not called the principal. He is called the vice-chancellor, and he is an Englishman. He is Professor Lancelot Hogben, from England."

By this time, Lena and Cholan were crossing the bridge into Lena's village. Lena said, "Please don't follow me any further. I will get into trouble."

"Okay. I will see you tomorrow in school. Goodbye." Cholan sprang on his bicycle and rode off toward Uitvlugt Front and his home. Lena walked the remainder of the way very briskly.

Mangri was on the front porch waiting. The other children were at her side. She looked through the windows between spoonfuls, as she fed Radhi, who was two years old, in 1962. Lena entered the house. She said, "Good afternoon, Ma," and put down her book bag. She was sweating from both fear and the tropical heat. It was 3:45 p.m., and the sun had made the streets shimmer with heat that oozed off from the crushed stones and bitumen that surfaced them. Lena opened her handkerchief and wiped the sweat from her face, forehead, and neck.

Mangri asked, "Where were you all the while? You know that these children came home by themselves?"

"I was in school. I was kept back by one of the teachers who wanted to explain something to me" Lena replied.

"Explain something to you! Were you alone, or was it the whole class?"

"I was alone. He asked me to remain after school. The headmaster was also nearby with his common entrance class."

"What is the name of this teacher?"

"Mr. Cholan. He is new. He assists my class teacher."

"Cholan! What Cholan? I only know of Mr. Warren Horton, who is your class teacher."

"Mr. Cholan Nauth is new. He is from Uitvlugt Front, and he said his father is the Pandit," Lena said.

"I know his parents," said Mangri skeptically. "Yes, his father is that businessman out there with the drooping bushy mustache. He is the man they call boiler-brush!"

Mangri, much more concerned now, said after she saw Lena smile, "Girl, this is not a joking matter. That young teacher should not ask you to remain alone, even if the headmaster was around. Those people are a troublesome lot. All the brothers and sisters of Cholan's mother live around. Her parents are also alive, and the children are fighting each other, and the parents, over poverty. I have to tell you father about this. Now, run along and take your shower. After that, I want you to come and help me in the kitchen with dinner."

Lena left. She was confused. First, Cholan and his talk about his dream, and now her mom and her talk about his family's problems. "Who cares?" she asked herself. "They have nothing to do with me," she felt.

That evening, after Baboo had eaten, and while he was working on his sewing machine, Mangri told him. Baboo was nonchalant. He said in reply, "Why worry? The young guy probably wants to help her. If there is any problem, Mr. Horton will tell me. Sometimes I see him in the bar on Friday evenings when I meet my friends for a drink." Baboo dismissed the matter. Something nagged at the back of Mangri's mind. She didn't know why. She was worried.

Cholan kept Lena for two other evenings after school. He helped her with reading and mathematics.

Baboo met Mr. Horton on Friday evening. They exchanged the usual greetings, but Mr. Horton did not mention anything to him. Baboo decided to ask about the new teacher. He approached Mr. Horton at the bar and said, "Excuse me, sir, I will like to find out something."

"Sure, Baboo! What is bothering you?" Mr. Horton asked. Mr. Horton sipped his beer. Baboo ordered a round for himself and Mr. Horton. Mr. Horton thanked Baboo. They cheered to each other's health. After Baboo had sipped, he said, "Mr. Horton, it is about my daughter, Lena. My wife told me that she came home from school late on three evenings during this week. Did you give her permission to have extra tuition after school?"

"No, Baboo! I am not aware of what you are saying! You have taken me by surprise with that information." Mr. Horton seemed a bit ruffled with the news.

Baboo continued, "I questioned my daughter, and she said that you have a new assistant teacher in your class. She said his name is Cholan, and he has been keeping her back in school in the evenings."

"Baboo, I did not know about this, man. I will look into the matter on Monday morning. If what you say is the truth, then I will have to caution that young man for giving evening lessons without my permission." Mr. Horton was embarrassed.

"I am very sorry to upset you at this time, Mr. Horton," Baboo apologized.

"No, man, don't apologize. It is your duty to find out what is going on! It's your child, and you should be interested," Mr. Horton replied.

"Thank you. Would you send me a note with Lena on Monday evening and let me know what is the decision?" Baboo asked.

"Sure, Baboo. I will do that."

Baboo ordered another round of beers. He wished Mr. Horton a pleasant evening. They drank and chatted about the country's politics. After a while, Baboo left for home.

Mr. Horton wrote Baboo a letter on Monday. Lena delivered it to her father. Baboo read:

> Uitvlugt Church of Scotland School
> West Coast Demerara
> May 20, 1962
> Dear Baboo,
>
> I spoke to Mr. Cholan today, and he said that he kept in Lena three evenings last week to help her in mathematics and reading. He said he felt that she needed help in these subjects for her pupil teacher certificate examinations. I told him that he was wrong to have kept her back without consultation with me. He apologized and said that he would like to help her and other students who have to take the same examination.
>
> I late spoke to the headmaster about this matter, and he agreed that Cholan should hold per-session classes on the condition that he takes all the examination students. Cholan has agreed to the headmaster's decision. It is now for you to decide whether Lena could remain for the evening class.
>
> Sincerely yours,
> Warren Horton

Baboo was pleased with the information contained in Mr. Horton's letter. He read it to Mangri, who was illiterate. He also discussed the contents with Lena. He asked her, "Do you want to remain for extra lessons in school after official dismissal?"

"Yes, Daddy. I want to pass my examinations. If the other kids remain, I will be very happy to join them. I am very much afraid to stay alone," Lena said.

Baboo smiled, "That's very good, Lena. I have already bought all your textbooks. They were very expensive. I do want you to pass your examinations. If any other textbooks are required for the evening lessons, then let me know. I will be very happy to get you all that you need. What do you think, Mangri?"

"I don't know, Baboo. Lena is now a young lady, and she has to be very careful. It is that Pandit's son...and the people are not saying good things about them. She has to be very careful and always try to be in the company of the other students," Mangri cautioned. Lena was looking at her parents when they spoke.

She said, "Daddy, I will try to do my best."

"You better do! I will like to see you graduate and to be somebody important when you grow up. Your elder sister, Mona, is already settled and is doing fine. She did not get the chance to go on to high school. However, I want you to go higher learning and to set an example for your other brothers and sisters to follow. As you have said, try to do your best," encouraged Baboo.

Mangri said, "Well, I think she understands what has to be done, Baboo. Let us leave that as it is. I want Lena to help me in the kitchen now, or you will have no dinner, Baboo!"

"Don't joke, lady! No dinner! I could eat a horse now." Baboo smiled.

"Sharpen your teeth then while we are cooking," Mangri retorted.

Lena continued having extra help in school from Monday to Thursday each week. Cholan had officially started his evening class with the guidance of Mr. Horton. Cholan now had fifteen students to tutor in the evenings. They were all taking the pupil-teachers examinations. Cholan had not expected this, but he was given no chance to bargain. The headmaster told him, without any reservations, "Since you have started to tutor one, you can tutor them all in the evenings. It seems that you are an ambitious young man, and you have started here with a bright new idea. I am very proud of you, Mr. Cholan. Mr. Horton said that if you tutor all of the exam students, then they will have a better chance to pass the examinations. Congratulations for your marvelous idea, Mr. Cholan!"

Cholan knew that Mr. Hull was very sarcastic, but he could not back out. His job was at stake. Instead, he said, "Thank you very much, Mr. Hull, for having so much confidence in me. I am looking forward to helping all the students. It will give me great pleasure, sir."

"That's very good of you, young man. In that way, you will be doing a great service to your community. You will be helping these students do better academically. By the way, Mr. Cholan, before you begin this evening class, I want you to get written consent from the parents of all the kids who will be attending. I will like to see those consent letters on my desk as early as possible," instructed Mr. Hull in a condescending tone.

"Yes, sir. I will inform the students to tell their parents to send in their consent letters," Cholan replied.

Baboo had replied to Mr. Horton's letter. His reply was accepted as his written consent to allow Lena to be in the class. Baboo had written:

> 126 Ocean View Uitvlugt
> West Coast Demerara May 21, 1962
>
> Dear Mr. Horton,
>
> The contents of your letter were read carefully and discussed among Lena, her mother, and me. We are very glad that other students will now be in the class. Let the headmaster know that we are very grateful to him for encouraging the formation of this class. We do know that the students will benefit a great deal. Lena

said that she will be happy to continue in the class. Both my wife and I have agreed that she should do so.

Once more, thank you very much.

Sincerely yours,
Baboo Arjune

Cholan worked sincerely, at first, with the students, and they were all eager to learn. As Cholan became more popular in the school, he started to befriend a young beautiful teacher named Rita Romain. Rita was one year younger than Cholan. She would often wait on Cholan until his evening class had dismissed. For Cholan, it was love at first sight. Cholan had not hesitated. On the very first occasion that he met Rita, he told her, "You are a very beautiful and charming young woman, Rita. I am very happy that I met you. I want to let you know that I love you!"

Rita was flattered. She replied, "How can you say that? How can you say you love me when you hardly even know me?"

It was at a teachers' conference on a Friday evening in late May of 1962. Cholan had sat near to Rita at the conference, and he was whispering in her ear as the headmaster boringly droned away at his messages to the faculty. "I know you well. From the very first day I joined the staff, I have seen you. I loved you instantly. I am even jealous. I have seen that old fool, Mr. Sookdeo, trying to talk to you," he finished with clenched teeth.

Rita blushed. "You have noticed a lot. I am not interested in Mr. Sookdeo. He is too old and worn out. Look at the very way he wears his clothing!" she ended with distaste in her voice.

"Don't kill the old fool. Play along with him. Flatter his ego, but remember I love you," Cholan said mischievously.

"You are a wicked guy," she chided. "You sound so sure of yourself," she teased.

Mr. Hull, in the middle of a new point about the pastor of St. Luke's Church that was located in the school's compound, paused and looked their way. They stopped whispering. Mr. Hull had not overheard them. He was not bothered by their whisperings. He had paused for want of better words, and in doing so, he looked around at the faculty. He almost immediately resumed talking.

Cholan slipped his hand under the desk, and he held Rita's hand. He half expected her to pull away her hand, but she didn't. Having been encouraged by her positive attitude, he lovingly caressed her hand with his. He whispered in her ear again, "Do you have anything to do on Saturday?"

"No! Why?"

"If you don't, then would you go to the cinema with me in Georgetown? We could have lunch first at a beautiful restaurant, then we could sneak in a 1:00 p.m. show at one of the cinemas," he suggested in a pleading tone.

"From your speech, you sounded as if you are very familiar with Georgetown. Are you?" she asked.

Rita was a buxom beauty with an oval face and long black hair combed backward over her shoulders. When she smiled, she revealed slenderly curved lips and well-formed lily-white teeth. It was pleasant to watch her smile. Cholan was captivated by her charming beauty.

He said, "Yes. I know Georgetown well, and I also know the cinemas. My uncle---that is, my mother's brother---is the cinema magnate in Georgetown. He owns most of the cinemas."

"Well, well! You are not only smart. You also come from a rich background." She chuckled lightly.

The headmaster was concluding his meeting, Cholan whispered to her, "We will walk down the street together after the meeting is ended. What do you say?"

"It's all right with me," she replied. He gave her hand a friendly squeeze, then released it. She looked at him and blushed.

The headmaster dismissed the faculty. The meeting had adjourned. Cholan and Rita left the school together. They pushed their bicycles as they walked. Cholan told her, "I'll walk all the way to Zeeburg with you, if you don't mind."

"No, I do not mind at all! As a matter of fact, I appreciate your company," she replied.

"Do you have any boyfriend, Rita?"

"No one particularly in whom I am interested," she said. He looked at her, stumbled, hitting his ankle on the bicycle's pedal.

"That's very nice to know. We could therefore get together more often."

"Sure, as you wish. I don't like to be bothered by Mr. Sookdeo, and he is so much older than I am," Rita encouraged. As she walked, she kept brushing her hair from her face and eyes. The cooling Atlantic breeze that fanned the coastland made the evening walk very comfortable. It was not a very humid evening, and the clouds threw a great shadow on the land, sheltering the public road from the evening rays of the declining sunshine. The wind had a smooth, steady gust about fifteen miles per hour as it was pushed by the washing tide from the Atlantic Ocean.

The public road on which Cholan and Rita walked ran parallel to the Atlantic Ocean, which washed the coastland. It was separated from the concreted seawall of the Atlantic to the north, by a distance of about two hundred yards of flat alluvial coastland clay.

"I am very happy that you do not have a boyfriend. I love you, and I want to know you better," Cholan continued, knowing he had made a conquest."

"To be honest, I also like you. It will be a pleasure for us to get together," she said.

"Very good! What are your hobbies or interests?" he asked.

"Oh! Not very much. I do read a lot. I borrow books from the library on various topics. Sometimes, in my spare time, I listen to music. When I am less bored, I try to study for my examinations. I am trying very hard to get acceptance at the Teacher's Training College. I want to be Class 1 Grade 1 trained teacher," she had replied.

"I am very happy to know that. You are very ambitious! On the other hand, I do not want to go to the Teacher's Training College. I want to attend the University of Guyana to get my bachelor's degree." He tried not to sound boastful.

Rita replied, "That is also very ambitious. You have all to gain and nothing to lose. You already have the entrance requirements, and you have youth. I wish you good luck.'

"I also wish you well. I do hope that you will be successful in gaining entrance to the college," he encouraged.

"I will. If you put your mind to something and work towards it, the possibility of success will be high," Rita replied.

"That's the way to think! I do congratulate you for your sound thoughts, and I wish you success," he said.

"Thank you." She blushed. "May we both be successful." She looked at him and blushed again.

They had reached her home. He wished her goodbye, saying "I will see you tomorrow in school. Tonight, I will dream about you." Rita laughed. "Bye!" she said.

On the following Saturday, Cholan and Rita crossed with the 9:15 ferry to Georgetown. They had taxied to Vreed en Hoop, separately. They met at the ferry stelling, crossed the Demerara River, and arrived in Georgetown at 10:00 a.m. They held hands as they disembarked from the ferry.

When they had met at Vreed en Hoop, Cholan had told her, "Thank you for showing up. You have made my day! You look very pretty this morning. I will get very jealous as other guys sneak looks at you today."

She had smiled. "Don't flatter me! You also look well!"

As they crossed the Demerara River, they chatted freely, like old friends. They stood on the bow, bracing on the rails and looking across the river to Georgetown's coastland. The large ferryboat, the *Atakouria*, rode the slightly choppy waters of the river like a colossal traversing surefootedly on known grounds. The huge British- manufactured passenger steamer had been plying the same waters for over a decade.

Cholan pointed to a mammoth bauxite carrier, The *Saguenay*, that was moored at midstream, and close to the mouth of the Demerara River, that emptied its water into the Atlantic. He said, "Could you imagine those huge ocean-going vessels sailing down the murky waters of this river, following in midchannel to the bauxite mines in Linden?"

"It's all left to the imagination, Cholan!" She looked at the huge ship that towered about one hundred feet above the water's surface. She continued, "The reason why the ship is moored out there is because the water is falling in the Atlantic. She is awaiting high tide, when maneuverability downstream will be more manageable."

"You are sure right," Cholan said. "The ships look beautiful moored along the wharves of Georgetown!"

They looked across at the many oceangoing vessels and the fishing trawlers that were moored there. There was a beautiful array of vessels, in different sizes. As the ferry approached the Georgetown stelling on the right bank of the Demerara River, they saw huge cranes on those ships, either loading or unloading their cargoes along the wharves on either side of the ferry stelling.

The *Makouria* moored. The passengers disembarked. Cholan and Rita, hand in hand, plodded their way along the busy shopping area of America Street and the Stabroek Market. This crowded are in Georgetown is called the Avenues of the Americas.

Cholan and Rita walked along Water Street, dodging in and out of crowds until they reached Regent Street. They walked along Regent Street, going cast, window-shopping along the way. They walked into Correia's jewelry store. Cholan bought Rita a gold ginger ring. She protested when she realized the purpose for entering the store. However, he insisted that she accepted the gift. After some more protests and reluctance, she tried on the ring. It fits snugly. She finally accepted the gift.

Cholan smiled. Rita thanked him. They continued walking along Regent Street until they reached the National Restaurant. It was lunchtime. They went in and took a table. The waiter approached, greeted them, and presented them the menu. They read the menu and looked up at each other.

Cholan said, "Well, what would you like to have?"

Rita replied, "I don't really have a choice. I will have the same that you will order."

Cholan selected. "Let's see. I will take a pork lo mein and a serving of roast pork at the side. I will wash down with a Banks beer. Now, do you eat pork?"

"Yes, I eat pork, but instead of a beer, I will take a Guinness stout," Rita said.

Cholan beckoned the waiter. He doubled his selection in the order, for them both. They sipped on their beverages while they waited their food. Cholan caressed Rita's hand under the table. "I love you," he told her. His breath caught. He breathed a sigh of relief.

She looked around the restaurant. Almost all the tables were occupied. There were many couples deeply engrossed in conversations or friendly bantering. There were also larger tables with groups of people, either families or friends. They were sharing jokes as they ate. The restaurant had the atmosphere of friendliness and relaxation. No one paid any attention, in particular, to any other table. Cholan and Rita sipped and enjoyed each other's company.

The soup came first, followed by their meal. They ate with leisure, savoring the meal. Cholan tried to make small talk as they ate. He said, "I love to eat here. This restaurant has a special recipe for its roast pork. It's always very delicious."

"I tend to agree with you. It is indeed very tasty," she commented. When they were about halfway through the meal, Cholan asked, "Which cinema have you selected? Do you want to go to any particular show?"

"No! Any show will suit me fine. I love to go to Metropole. We could walk from there to the ferry after the show. No, I have not selected a particular show. I want to get there and relax," Rita suggested.

"Then to the Metropole Cinema we will go," Cholan concluded.

They finished the rest of the meal in silence, after which Rita went to the washroom. Cholan paid the bill, then went to the men's room.

Together they walked hand in hand to the movie. Cholan bought the tickets to balcony seats of the cinema. The cinema had three levels of seating arrangements, as was common with every cinema in Guyana. At the lower level was the largest seating area. This was called the pit. The seats were rows of long wooden benches, with two aisles separating the three rows of seats. The middle level was called the house and was about four feet higher than the pit. Its seats were cushioned. The upper level was called the balcony. No fan from the pit or the house could see in the balcony. The balconies of the cinemas were popularly known as the lovers' lanes. The Metropole's balcony was dark and cozy.

Cholan hugged Rita very closely when they had sat down. She didn't protest. He ventured forward, and with his lips he sought hers. She yielded to his embrace and his roving lips on her face. They kissed, and at that moment, they were oblivious to all around them. Other couples were also engaged in similar activities. Cholan's main idea was not to see the movie, but to use the occasion to make love to Rita. On his first date, he was achieving his goal. Rita did not negate his advances.

As he caressed her face, neck, and body and kissed her, he whispered to her that he loved her. She replied that she also loved him. Before the movie had ended, he told her, nibbling at her ears, "Rita, you are charming, beautiful, and irresistible. I love you and I want to make love to you!"

"No! I am afraid. Someone may see us and spread the news around!" she replied.

"Don't be scared. We are far away from home. No one knows us here. I will find a place!" he encouraged.

"Where would we go?" she asked.

"Don't you worry your pretty head. I know of a motel in Regent Street!" His voice caught.

She looked at him in the semidarkness and said, "Okay. Let us leave before the show is ended. I do not know who is in the crowd. I don't want to be seen by anyone who may know me."

"As you wish. Let's go," he replied. They stood up, hand in hand. He led her through the aisle of the balcony to the exit. When they stepped outside of the cinema, they shaded and blinked their eyes until they had become adjusted to the brilliant glare of the sun. The asphalted street shimmered with tropical heat.

Cholan hailed a cab. When they stepped in, he gave directions. The cab sped through Georgetown and up the east coast to the Carib Motel. It was at Lilendaal, three miles out of Georgetown. The cab took thirty minutes to reach its destination. The Carib Motel was a three-floor wooden structure painted in white and silhouetted in an open expanse of beautiful landscape, on the southern side of the public road at Lilendaal. On the northern side of the public road, and beyond a hundred feet of flatlands was the sprawling Atlantic Ocean, with its murky coastland waters.

When Cholan and Rita stepped out of the cab in front of the motel, they felt the spray of water as they lashed upon the sturdy concreted seawall that was built to prevent the coastlands from being flooded by the Atlantic high tides. They smelled the freshness of the Atlantic trade winds and tasted the salt in the sprays.

Cholan paid the smiling cabdriver and hurriedly led Rita into the motel's lobby. He hurried away so as to avoid being recognized by passing cabdrivers and passengers. At the desk, Cholan paid for a room for an hour's usage.

As they entered the room, Rita asked, with concern in her voice, "How do you know about this place? It's out of Georgetown."

"Some friends and I went to look at the campus of the University of Guyana, which is now under construction. On our way home, we stopped in at the Carib. The university's buildings are being constructed at Turkeyen, two miles farther up on the east coast," Cholan answered.

"Now that you know of this place, it will suit you right! You could bring your other women here, women that you would pick up when you start classes at the Turkeyen campuses," she persisted with a woman's jealousy.

He took her in his arms, embraced her, and whispered, "Stop worrying your head about things that haven't started as yet. I have no other women, only you, my beautiful." He kissed her, stopping any further complaints. She resisted for a short moment, then rapidly yielded completely. They made love.

They discovered each other's sexuality. They separately realized that the other was not a virgin. They did not discuss this after, locked away in their minds. After making love, Cholan tried to reassure the blushing Rita. He wanted her to feel that they had not sinned. He wanted to get rid of her guilt. He said, "Do not feel ashamed. No one has seen us. We are lovers!" He held her in his arms for some time.

She did not reply. She quietly dressed, combed her long beautiful hair, and made her face. Quietly they stepped out of the motel and through the entrance to the public road. Gone was the earlier exuberance and excitement! Their only thought was to be as far away from the motel as quickly as possible. They walked down the road, side by side, for a few hundred yards, in the westerly direction, toward Georgetown. They stopped and hailed a passing taxi. They stepped in the cab, not saying anything. Rita looked through the window to her left. Cholan reached out and held her hand onto the seat of the cab. He squeezed it gently, releasing and squeezing again. She looked at him quickly and turned away. She smiled. He drew closer and held her in his left arm.

The cabbie quickly looked through his rearview mirror. Cholan was oblivious of the cabbie's presence. He gently turned Rita's face toward him and kissed her. She responded. After a long moment, he released her.

He observed that they were in Georgetown, traveling along Brickdam, and quickly approaching the ferry stelling. Rita took her brush, looked in her pocket mirror, and fixed her hair. She applied her lipstick and powdered her face and nose. By the time she was finished with her paraphernalia, the cab had reached the Georgetown car park. Cholan paid the driver. They stepped out and casually walked toward the stelling, window-shopping on the way. At the Stabroek Market, they stopped at a florist, and he bought her a bunch of roses.

She accepted with pleasure. Side by side they boarded the ferry, speaking casually. No one greeted them as they wended their way passengers to the stern of the ferry. They proceeded to among the stern seats close to the guard rails. Their conversation continued in whispered tones. Cholan told her, "No one seem to notice us so far. If we are recognized, anyone may think that we have bumped into each other accidentally."

"That's the way I want it to be. Do not sit too close to me, but you could keep the conversation going," she replied.

He said, "I love you. I enjoyed today. What about you?"

"I enjoyed it too, but let's change the subject. When would you start out at the university, and what course you expect to pursue?"

"I want to do my BA, majoring in foreign languages. I love Spanish. I have decided that Spanish will be my major," Cholan answered.

"That sounds interesting. We have many Spanish-speaking countries in the continent. Also, it will be an asset to you because they have now introduced the subject in the schools," expostulated Rita, trying to impress him with her knowledge of what's happening in the educational spectrum of the society.

"You surely have that right. There are not many Spanish teachers around, and soon, there may be a great demand for these personnel, as the subject gains acceptance across the country," Cholan replied.

"I agree with you. They have included the language in the Broadcasts to Schools program," she enlightened him, referring to the daily radio broadcasts to the schools' population.

The ferry had unmoored and was routed across the Demerara River. They looked at the beautiful line of vessels along the wharves. Rita commented, "It's never boring to watch these ships. I wonder what it is like to be working at sea!"

"Ah! That's another domain that needs exploring," he said. "I think one has to love sailing and traveling to be a sailor. Also, one has to love the sea. That's not for me. I can't swim!" Cholan concluded.

Rita laughed. "That makes two of us," she said.

They disembarked at Vreed en Hoop and took a taxi home.

Cholan bade her goodbye when he got off at Uitvlugt. Rita traveled on to the neighboring village, Zeeburg, and to her home.

Cholan and Rita met again at work on Monday morning. They were eager to see each other. They walked to an end room and stood behind a mobile chalkboard. No other teacher or students were nearby.

School was not set as yet. The students were playing in the schoolyard. The teachers were in the staffroom.

Cholan embraced Rita behind the screen and quickly kissed her. She responded, then shoved him away. "You fool! You want to get us into trouble! You have to be careful!"

"Ah! No one will see us," he nervously responded.

"Have you heard that walls have eyes? Someone may see us here at the rear of the school, and they will put two and two together! The rumors will begin, and we will both be in hot water," she continued.

"Ah, who cares about us?" he asked.

"You never know!"

The bell rang. They proceeded to their classrooms the receive the students.

Mr. Sookdeo, on his way to his classroom, espied Cholan and Rita returning to their classes. A streak of anger burned his heart. Mr. Sookdeo roughly threw his briefcase on his table and welcomed his class with a gruff, "Good morning, boys and girls. Take out your notebooks and head up for mental arithmetic, numbers 1 to 25. Remember, if you are caught cheating, you will be given six strokes instantly with the wild cane."

When these strokes were administered by the teacher, the girls were caned on the palms on their hands and the boys were lashed across their buttocks. Sometimes, when the girls could take no more lashes on their palms, they would request to be caned on their buttocks. Mr. Sookdeo would take great pleasure to spank the skirts of the girls and stroke them with the wild cane across their buttocks. Mr. Sookdeo loved to hear the girls cry out in pain.

That morning, the students paid the consequences for Mr. Sookdeo's jealousy. They received one lash with the cane for every mental arithmetic problem that was worked wrong. At the end of the period, some of the boys were literally unable to sit. Many of the girls were unable to hold their pens to write. Constantly during the beatings, Mr. Sookdeo took out his handkerchief and wiped the sweat off his forehead and brows.

The other classes near Mr. Sookdeo's were very quiet around as his lesson, intermixed with corporal punishment, progressed. That afternoon after school was dismissed, Mr. Sookdeo remained at his desk, pretending to work on class records. Rita also remained in her class, pretending to study. Cholan worked with his examinations students, as was usual.

Sometime after Cholan's class had started, Rita came over and sat at the back of his room. Cholan acknowledged her presence and continued with his work. As the students worked, Rita asked, "Could I assist you to check their work, Mr. Cholan? I would like to remain and help."

"Sure, you may do so, miss. I am very happy to have your help," Cholan replied.

Rita moved from student to student, checking and helping them with their work. The lesson progressed smoothly. The examinations students were happy to have additional tutoring by the young and beautiful Miss Rita.

In the meantime, Mr. Sookdeo passed by several times, glancing at Cholan and Rita working together. Mr. Sookdeo burned with anger. He felt like choking Cholan to death. However, he suffused his rage and waited. Cholan dismissed his class, because of the additional help, before the scheduled time. After the students had departed, Cholan and Rita left together, pushing their cycles as they engaged in their lovers' conversation.

Mr. Sookdeo watched them from afar. He followed slowly, riding on his bicycles, jealousy and hate welling in his heart. For the next couple of weeks that followed, Cholan and Rita became more obvious to the onlooker in their love affair. The staff knew that they were lovers, and Mr. Sookdeo accosted Cholan.

It happened one Friday evening after school was out. Mr. Sookdeo stopped Cholan, as Cholan and Rita were leaving the schoolyard. Mr. Sookdeo came face-to-face with them, addressing Cholan, "Why don't you leave my woman alone, Cholan? I intend to marry Rita. We were making progress towards marriage before you joined the staff!"

"It is not my intention to steal your woman, Mr. Sookdeo. However, if you are referring to Rita, well, she told me that she has no boyfriends," Cholan replied.

Rita seethed with anger. She said, "Who are you two guys to discuss me as if I am of no significance? And who told you that I am your woman, Mr. Sookdeo? I am nobody's woman. Let us get that clear!"

A crowd of teachers stood by, listening. They were on their way home, but having overheard the confrontation, they lingered close by to catch every word that was said. They felt it would be a weekend treat and looked forward to what they would later call the juiciness of the matter.

"Do not deny me, Rita!" Mr. Sookdeo said angrily. "You and I had an affair for a long time!" He looked at his gathering colleagues and pointed at them. "All these teachers can testify to that, Rita."

The teachers said nothing. They listened.

Cholan shouted, pointed at Sookdeo, "Look, man! Don't scandal Rita like that! You ought to be ashamed of yourself!"

"I am not scandalling's her name! We have been going steady for a long while! We dated many times. We went further than dating. We---"

Sookdeo didn't finish recounting his intimacies with Rita. With his right fist, Cholan struck Sookdeo solidly on the mouth. Sookdeo's lips pulped. Blood dripped on his tie and shirt front. The teachers gasped.

Sookdeo saw the blood and raged. He screamed, "You bastard, you dare to strike me!" Sookdeo sprang at Cholan. He grabbed Cholan by the throat and squeezed with all his strength. Cholan staggered backward, then regained his balance. As he gasped for breath, he struck Sookdeo in the midsection. He scratched Sookdeo's face, clawing at his eyes. He tried desperately to loosen Sookdeo's hands, but to no avail. He raised his right knee and struck Sookdeo's scrotum. Sookdeo winced with pain, released Cholan's throat, and folded up, going down slowly on the dusty ground. Cholan rubbed his throat, panting for breath. He bent forward, gasping and choking as he inhaled deeply.

Sookdeo glared at Cholan, the blood clotting on his battered lips. He stood up quickly and sprang at Cholan. The force of his action caused them both to go down, Sookdeo on top of Cholan. Sookdeo straddled Cholan, burying his knees in the ground. He turned in a semi twist to the right, from waist up, and drew back his right fist, aiming to descend like a sledgehammer on Cholan's face. His insanity was beyond controlling. He only wanted to pound the face under him. He wanted to shatter, as he felt, that pompous younger man under him. Cholan wriggled, jerked upward, and pushed at Sookdeo's body, but he couldn't dislodge him. Cholan groaned in anger and desperation. Sookdeo grunted in hate. As his fist flashed through the air and began the descent, Mr. Horton's tall figure plunged and grabbed Sookdeo's arm. He instantaneously yanked Sookdeo off Cholan and said, "Stop this, Sookdeo. You are a big man and a trained teacher! Quit this nonsense!" Another male teacher stepped in and helped Cholan to his feet. The fight had gone out of Cholan. He was trembling, scared.

On the other hand, Sookdeo tried to get out of Horton's grasp. He couldn't manage the bigger man. Slowly, his anger subsided. After a while, Mr. Horton released him. Cholan was almost through the gate in the company of the other male teacher.

Mr. Horton led Sookdeo to the fountain. Sookdeo calmly washed his hands, then methodically began to wash the blood off his face and neck. He soaked his handkerchief and tried to wipe the blood off his shirt. He did not get much off. The water made the stains larger. Sookdeo, through the advice of Mr. Horton, took his shirt off and washed it at the fountain. Mr. Sookdeo looked at Mr. Horton. "I didn't start the fight! It was that punk who struck me in the face!" he said.

"We saw and heard it all, Mr. Sookdeo. It was disgraceful! You guys ought to be ashamed of yourselves, and you are lucky that the kids were not around to see this," Mr. Horton sternly commented.

When the fight has started, Rita looked on in shock and saw the first exchanges. She felt ashamed and disgraced. She climbed on her bicycle and swiftly rode away. The tears of anger were blinding her eyes. She blinked her eyes constantly as she rode in the sun toward the western horizon and her home.

Mr. Horton continued, "As a senior master, I have to report this matter on Monday morning to the headmaster, because you have fought on the school's premises. I'll say, man, it's disgraceful!"

Mr. Sookdeo defended, much more calmly, "You know that I was courting Rita for a long time now. She started avoiding me when that fool joined us. I know his kind! He is only fooling around with her, and she is too blind to see it. I had loved her, but after this, I don't know anymore!" Sookdeo's emotions saddened. He felt despair, as his pented anger ebbed.

The other teachers who had milled around during the confrontation had dispersed in twos and threes with the topic hot on their lips. They surmised what may have happened between Rita and each of her lovers. They joked about their imaginary sexual encounters with her. Rita had now become the laughingstock of the staff. Cholan, they felt, was a young man to be watched.

Mr. Horton walked with Mr. Sookdeo. Mr. Sookdeo had put away his bloody shirt in his bag. His face was clean. The bleeding had stopped. His lips were swollen, but not very noticeable. The cooling water of the fountain had prevented much swelling. In his vest, Mr. Sookdeo looked like a regular Friday afternoon volleyball player who had done a thorough practice in the blazing sunshine.

They stopped in the nearest textile store. Mr. Sookdeo bought a dress shirt, then proceeded home. As they approached the first bar on the way, Mr. Horton said, "Come in and have a drink with me, Mr. Sookdeo. A double shot of El Dorado Bonded Reserve Rum will do you good! What do you say?"

"I think after all that happened this evening, I need that drink, Mr. Horton! Let's go!" Mr. Sookdeo replied, with much enthusiasm.

As was usual on Friday afternoons, the bar was crowded with sugar workers. Friday was pay day at Uitvlugt sugar plantation, and it was customary among most of the workers to imbibe in their alcoholic revelry before they took their pay home. As a consequence, very often, on Friday evenings, many wives would be seen visiting liquor restaurants and bars, looking for their husbands to relieve them of adequate cash to manage the home. In many instances, if the wives do not show up to demand money, the men, in their drunken stupor, would exhaust their weekly pay pockets.

Sugar workers are large consumers of Demerara Rum, of which there are international winnings blends such as XM 10 Years Old, XM Gold Medal, and El Dorado Bonded Reserve. Very much alcohol is consumed by these workers, and when they gather for their weekend drinks, as much as forty ounces of rum would be consumed by two men drinking together on a Friday evening spree.

On entering the bar, amid high-pitched conversations and a smoke-filled interior, Mr. Horton espied a vacant corner table overlooking the public road that was the main road for trafficking on the coastland. Having claimed the table for the evening by resting their bags on the tabletop, Mr. Horton and Mr. Sookdeo walked over to the ordering counter. On the way there, Mr. Horton asked, "What would you have, Mr. Sookdeo?"

"I don't really know! I don't have a choice. I will drink whatever you choose," Mr. Sookdeo replied.

"Would you prefer vodka, gin, or rum?" insisted Mr. Horton.

"I think I will have rum."

"In that case," Mr. Horton said, "we will take a twenty-four-ounce bottle of Bonded Reserve!" Mr. Horton was a copious consumer of alcohol. He always looked forward to weekends when he would indulge, sometimes to a drunken stupor.

Mr. Sookdeo, however, was an infrequent drinker, but on that evening, he felt like getting drunk. Mr. Horton took his rum, Coke, glasses with ice, cigarettes, and cubed cheese with hot sauce to the table. Mr. Sookdeo followed with a bottle of cold water. They rinsed their glasses and lavishly poured the rum on the ice. They added Coke to the iced rum and shook the contents of the glasses, making the rhythmical clinking music of ice rattling on glass.

Mr. Horton raised his glass. "To you, Mr. Sookdeo, may you win the girl!"

"I do not know anymore whether I want to win, Mr. Horton. Anyway, to your health, and thanks," said Mr. Sookdeo as he raised his glass. They clinked their glasses together. They drank deeply. Mr. Horton wiped his lips with the back of his left hand. He said, "Gosh, man, that's good!"

Mr. Sookdeo grimaced in pain. He replied, "Gosh, man, that burns!" He took out of his handkerchief and sopped up the alcohol from his damaged lips. The second drink burned Mr. Sookdeo a little less, but by the time he got down to the third drink, he didn't even feel a twang of pain. The alcohol had taken effect on Mr. Sookdeo's nervous system and numbed his injuries.

As they drank, Mr. Horton and Mr. Sookdeo discussed Cholan and Rita until they ran out of things to say. They then moved on to the current cricket series, the West Indies versus England, which was played at home on the West Indies. They argued about bowling, batting, and fielding. They clashed in heated, friendly arguments about who was the best cricket all-rounder, the best batsman, and the fastest bowler. They recounted, as they argued, facts and figures of each player under contention. It was amazing for the listener to hear these men discuss the statistics of international Test cricketers from their memory of what they had seen and read of these cricketers over the years. Most Guyanese and West Indies are human encyclopedias of cricketing history and Test records of games played among England and her former colonies and allies, such as New Zealand, Australia, India, Pakistan, Ceylon, Bangladesh, Zimbabwe, and the West Indies.

Most of the Guyanese cricketers were born and grew up on the sugar plantations, where the interest in cricket is high. Cricket sits on the lips of every sugar worker. By the time Mr. Horton and Mr. Sookdeo had exhausted their most popular topic, the twenty-four-ounce bottle had been depleted. Mr. Sookdeo was glowing with vigor and manliness. He felt that he could beat up two Cholans together. He stood up and puffed his chest, forgetting his chapped lips. He said to Mr. Horton, "You know, I wish could see that motherf---in here now. I will make minced meat with him!" He banged his fist on the table. The glasses rattled. Some of the inmates of the bar looked their way and whispered to their mates, "The teacher is getting sponged!" They laughed among themselves.

Mr. Horton said, "Come off that, man. You are too smart for such foolishness. It's your turn to get the other bottle. Go get it, man! Here is two dollars." He placed the money on the table. Mr. Sookdeo pushed the money in Mr. Horton's shirt pocket. "Keep your money, Mr. Horton. I have enough to get what we need." Mr. Sookdeo went and replenished the table.

When they poured their first drink from the second bottle, Mr. Horton asked, "What do you think of the political situation in Guyana?"

Politics was another ball game! It completed with cricket for first place among the Guyanese topical discussion.

"I don't know what is happening in the country! Instead of Blacks and Indians being united, day by day, they are drifting further and further apart," Mr. Sookdeo said with much bitterness.

"It's the British diplomacy. They are playing one race against another. They have always done that wherever they colonized. If it's not race, it's religion!" Mr. Horton compromised.

"I agree. They are cutting all the ties that our people have cultivated over the centuries, and we are drifting apart," said Mr. Sookdeo.

"Yes, we are drifting apart! It will not be good for this country!" lamented Mr. Horton, his speech slurring. He gulped down another large drink. He hiccupped and wiped his mouth. He said, "It is as it is, Mr. Sookdeo. Our ancestors, yes, our ancestors, the people of the two larger races in this country, used to live side by side of each other, like brothers. They lived in the villages together. But alas! The sixties had dawned with problems! Blacks and Indians are not united! And they are not seeing beyond their noses...yeah... their noses. The political leaders of their own race group! They are neglecting the bondage that had held them together, laying waste their integrated heritage! It's a sad moment in history for this country, Mr. Sookdeo!"

Mr. Horton wiped the tears streaming down his cheeks. Mr. Sookdeo, semi dazed with alcohol, touched Mr. Horton on the hand and said, "Let's not bother with the politics of this country now, Mr.

Horton. It...it is...too big a piece of cake for us. Let the politicians settle their differences. We have our own problems to solve. I have my own battle to fight! Say, Mr. Horton, would you like me to get us some black puddings and hot sauce? Man, I am getting hungry!"

"Sure, Mr. Sookdeo!" Mr. Horton said, much more in control of himself. "You should have suggested that a long time ago!" They both laughed. Mr. Sookdeo left to purchase the sausages.

Black pudding is a Guyanese delicacy. It is made with the blood and intestines of the cow, along with other ingredients such as boiled rice and spices. The entrails of the cattle are thoroughly cleaned. The boiled rice is mixed in the blood along with garlic, thyme, basil, black pepper, clove, spice, and salt. The seasonings or spices are added in liberal quantities for taste.

The mixture is then funneled into the cleaned entrails. Both ends of the entrail are tightly tied. The pudding is then boiled for about half an hour. Boiling the pudding is an intricate process. Overboiling will cause it to rupture and lay waste its contents in the water.

The black pudding seller, with his tray of delicacies perched on a makeshift table, was a welcome personage outside almost every bar or liquor restaurant in the countryside. Sookdeo bought two dollars' worth of puddings and requested much hot sauce. They emptied the last of their rum in their glasses, cheered each other, and gulped down their drinks. They shared the black pudding.

Having finished, Horton rubbed his tummy and belched heartily. He clapped Sookdeo on the shoulder. "That was good, man, very good. Let's go. We could get some more on our way out and take it to the beer garden for a final wash down with beers. What do you say, Sookdeo?"

"It sounds good to me," replied Sookdeo. "I feel like...like painting the town red tonight!"

They both laughed. They stood and staggered out of the liquor restaurant. At the door, the cooling evening wind blew across their faces and bodies. They staggered much more as they crossed the public road. They weaved in and out with their bicycles. But they were not satiated! They stopped at the first beer shop and called for two bottles of Bank beers. They ended up drinking three beers each. When they finally jumped on their cycles to ride home, both teachers made several attempts before they were finally mounted. Once mounted, they crisscrossed to the left and right for some distance before they gained proper balance.

The rest of the distance home was done in a heavily intoxicated state of mind. It was as if the bicycles were set on magnetic courses. Mr. Horton and Mr. Sookdeo managed to remain mounted, but they looked as if they were circus riders, weaving their way among pedestrians and traffic. It was a common scene of the weekend drunken bicyclists in the sugar belt of Guyana.

3

On the following Monday morning Rita did not speak to Cholan when they passed each other in the school's lobby. She felt extremely embarrassed to even make eye contact with him. Cholan, on the other hand, did not attempt to approach her either. He was too much preoccupied with his own predicament.

Before school was set, Mr. Horton had reported to Mr. Hull what had happened between Mr. Sookdeo and Mr. Cholan. Mr. Hull, on learning of the incident, was enraged. He immediately summoned an emergency staff meeting. At the meeting, Mr. Hull, in his anger, neglected to greet his staff with the usual salutation, "Good morning, ladies and gentlemen." Instead he said, when all the teachers were gathered, "I call these meeting because of what happened to Mr. Sookdeo and Mr. Cholan on Friday evening. I learnt that most of you were witnesses to the incident. I will not tolerate such disgraceful actions by my members of the staff. The two teachers in question ought to be ashamed of themselves." Mr. Sookdeo, at this point, raised his hand, indicating that he would like to speak. Mr. Hull became further enraged. He shouted, "Keep your hand down and let me finish. You should be ashamed of yourself, Mr. Sookdeo, as a senior teacher on this staff. I know that your stupid actions of Friday will be whispered around this community like wildfire spreading with the Atlantic winds! You two teachers involved ought to feel stupid of yourselves to scandal the name of one of my young female teachers in the open! Rita has always been a good worker and a colleague of us all!"

Mr. Hull had always liked Rita. She was his favorite student. He was very proud of her when she passed her pupil teachers examinations. He went all out to secure her employment on his staff. Mr. Hull looked at Rita and continued, "I want both of you fellows to stand up now and apologize to Rita!"

Mr. Hull glared at Mr. Sookdeo and Mr. Cholan. There was a brief silence. Cholan and Sookdeo looked at each other in anger and frustration. Mr. Sookdeo looked around at his colleagues, who were staring in his direction. He knew that the faculty expected him to make the first move, being the senior teacher involved.

Mr. Sookdeo's eyes made contact with Mr. Horton. Mr. Horton shook his head. Sookdeo slowly stood up, embarrassed. He spoke shakily, "Mr. Hull, it was not my intention to get into a fistfight with Mr. Cholan. I do know better now, and I am very sorry for what happened to Rita, and I want to say now that I was wrong to mention her name in the argument with Mr. Cholan. I am very sorry, Miss Rita, to have caused you pains and sufferings over the incident. Please accept my apology. I am sorry for all the inconvenience that I have caused you." Mr. Sookdeo looked at Miss Rita. She had her head bowed. She was looking at the floor. She nodded her head. Mr. Sookdeo slowly sat down and looked at Mr. Horton. Mr. Horton smiled. Mr. Sookdeo felt relieved.

All eyes turned to Mr. Cholan. He was debating in his mind whether he should stand and apologize. He felt that he had won. After all he already had Rita sexually, and the incident with Mr. Sookdeo was mainly caused when Mr. Sookdeo was trying to disgrace Miss Rita in the public.

With baited breath, the faculty waited. Mr. Hull broke the silence. He looked at Mr. Cholan and said, "Well, Mr. Cholan!"

Cholan took the cue. He felt that his job might be in jeopardy if he did not apologize. He proudly stood up and smiled. Mr. Hull looked at him and glowed in anger.

Smilingly, Cholan said, "Mr. Hull, ladies and gentlemen, it was an unfortunate incident that took place on Friday evening. I was merely trying to defend the honor of Miss Rita." He looked at her bowed head. He thought she was a sweet wretch! He pictured himself making love to her. He said, "I want to openly apologized to Miss Rita and to let her know that I deeply regretted the incident. I wish to continue being her friend and to have a working relationship with Mr. Sookdeo. I am sorry, Miss Rita, to have caused you distress and embarrassment." Cholan looked at Mr. Hull. He sat down.

Mr. Hull resumed talking. "I am not allowing this incident to pass very easily. I want both of you gentlemen to give me a signed statement by lunchtime today. I will place it in your personal files, and it will be used against you should there be a reoccurrence of this incident!" Mr. Hull looked at Mr. Sookdeo and Mr. Cholan consecutively. Both men caught his eyes and nodded in agreement.

Mr. Hull concluded, "We are now fifteen minutes late for the start of school. Get to your classes immediately and let's begin the day's work. Secretary, ring the bell."

They rushed off to their classes. School was set for the morning session. Cholan was uneasy during the day. He debated whether he should pursue his relationship with Rita. By evening he concluded that there was trouble in her direction. He did not want to have further problems with Mr. Sookdeo. He reasoned if it was true that Mr. Sookdeo loved Rita, then he felt that he should let her be so that Mr. Sookdeo could resume his flirtations with her.

Let the old fool have his way! Cholan smiled. After all, I have had her already. He gloated in triumph and looked toward Lena, working at her desk. There are greener pastures, he thought, and dismissed his affair with Rita.

Pertaining to relinquishing the affair with Cholan, Rita did not extend any amorous flirtations to him during that week or the weeks that followed. Their relationship remained cordial and professional. As the weeks passed, Cholan observed that Rita was gravitating toward Mr. Sookdeo. Cholan, with that knowledge, felt more comfortable and at ease to try to influence his student Lena and to win her confidence.

Lena, like most of her fellow senior students, was aware of Cholan's relationship with Rita. They had seen them kissing in hiding, in school, on many occasions. As senior students, at ages fourteen to sixteen, they had discussed this relationship among themselves. They had concluded that Rita and Cholan were having sex. They had also observed Mr. Sookdeo's interest in Rita and had seen Mr. Sookdeo's exhibition of anger when matters did not go his way. At various stages in the triangular relationship, as silent observers, the students had experienced happiness, jealousy, and sympathy for the teachers involved. The boys were happy for Mr. Cholan. The girls were jealous of Miss Rita. As students they were in sympathy with Mr. Sookdeo. Most times they hated Mr. Sookdeo as well, whenever they saw him in his anger and frustration, registering corporal punishment, to their fellow students.

Cholan continued working with his evening class, Miss Rita did not join him anymore, nor was he interested in her any longer. He contemplated gaining the attention of Lena. From time to time, as Lena worked, Cholan would deposit notes on little pieces of paper on her desk stating that he loved her. In the evenings as she walked home from school, he would escort her. Lena was much flattered when he told her one evening that he was in love with her.

She replied, "How could you when you are in love with Miss Rita??

He denied, "We were friends. I do not love her, and our friendship is now ended. You may have noticed that I do not see her, nor do we sit and chat anymore. I only love you, Lena!"

Lena was skeptical. She was confused. She tried to reason whether he was speaking the truth. She asked, "How could you love me when I am still a student and only fourteen years old?"

"One does not have to be older to be loved. You are a mature young lady, and you are beautiful! You are also very bright. I love you for all those things!" he persisted.

"Well, I don't know much about love. The title that I know is what I have read in novels," she said.

"You are not too young to learn. I do know that in time, you will grow to love me," he told her.

She was flabbergasted! How could this young man claim that he was in love with her? Of course, there are many other beautiful and older young ladies out there! Maybe he is lying, she thought.

She told him, "I do not know what to say. I do not understand this thing called love."

"Well, it's like when two people like one another and they want to share their lives together. They want to get married and have a family of their own," he tried to educate her.

"Who is talking about marriage?" she asked. "I am too young to get married! And what about my schooling? I still have examinations to write!" she said, much disturbed.

"You could do all that if we get married. I will be closer to you, and I will be able to help you much more!" As he spoke, he keenly looked at the expressions on her face. He thought that he was creating an impression on her young mind. He said, "I will like to marry you. What do you say?"

"I don't know! As I said, I am still in school. I don't know what to tell you!" She was extremely confused.

"I will tell you what," he said, "I will come home this weekend, on Saturday evening and speak to your parents. What do you say?"

"I don't know," she replied. "I am scared."

"Don't be frightened," he persisted. "All will work out well for us. I will speak to your parents on Saturday evening."

They were approaching her home. He wished her goodbye, climbed on his bicycle, and rode off. Lena walked home quietly, said "Good afternoon" to her mother and went to her room. She lay on her bed calmly and tried to clear her thoughts. As the minutes ticked away, she became further confused. In her state of mind, the tears trickled down her cheeks. She barely heard her mother calling to her. Quickly, she changed her clothing and joined her mom in the kitchen.

Mangri looked at her and said, "Is everything all right, Lena? Your eyes are red! Do you have a fever or a headache?"

"Yes, Ma. I have a headache," Lena replied.

"I will make you a hot cup of tea. You could drink it with two aspirins and go to bed. I will wake you later for dinner," Mangri said.

"Yes, Ma, I will go to bed," Lena said humbly.

On the following days of the week Cholan continued courting Lena in and out of school. She gradually began to accept the idea that Teacher Cholan loved her.

Mr. Horton, the class teacher, noticed Mr. Cholan's interest in Lena. He warned Cholan to keep away from the student. Cholan did not heed Mr. Horton's warnings. Instead, he continued escorting Lena on her way home every evening. Mr. Horton made a mental note of the situation and decided that he would speak to Baboo about the matter. Mr. Horton did not report to Mr. Cholan to Mr. Hull. He felt that Mr. Hull may take drastic actions against the young man. Mr. Horton further felt that Lena's father may be able to dissuade her against Mr. Cholan.

Mr. Horton, with Mr. Cholan in mind, dropped in on Friday evening at his usual liquor restaurant for his Friday revelry and drinking spree. Baboo, on his way from work, decided to stop by for a refreshing Banks beer. Baboo was surprised when Mr. Horton hailed him out. Baboo knew of Mr. Horton's drinking ability and did not want to be engaged in a long drinking session. He had wanted to get home after the beer to continue his work on the security clothing for which he had an urgent order from the sugar plantation's administrative manager.

Baboo had received the contract to sew for the security guards, and he wanted to push his best foot forward to impress the administrative manager. He wondered why Mr. Horton was calling him. Maybe, he thought, the gentleman was short of cash, and he needed a loan. In the past, Mr. Horton had asked him for small loans.

Baboo answered Mr. Horton and stepped over to the teacher's table. Mr. Horton was drinking, alone. He greeted Baboo, "How do you do, man? It's a long time since I last saw you! Were you hiding from me, Baboo?"

"No, Mr. Horton. I was not hiding from you. I am a very busy man, teach. I have lots of sewing to do, and time is short," said Baboo.

"Don't speak like that, Baboo! Time is never short! You speak as if you are going to die soon, Baboo! Are you sick, man?" cautioned, and asked, Mr. Horton.

"No! I don't mean death! I meant that I have lots of orders for clothing and very limited time in which to do the work," Baboo clarified.

"I think that you are overworking, Baboo. You need to relax, man. Sit down and loosen up!" Mr. Horton invited.

"I don't have the time to spare!" protested Baboo.

"There you go again! Sit down and let's have few drinks," coaxed Mr. Horton.

"Okay, you win! What the hell!" said Baboo.

Mr. Horton drank his El Dorado Bonded Reserve Rum. Baboo drank beers. They chatted about the latest cricket series and politics. When Baboo had finished his second beer, Mr. Horton said, "There is something I want to tell you, Baboo, and I need your help. It is probably for the good of your daughter Lena," Mr. Horton said.

Baboo was surprised. He did not expect Mr. Horton to speak of Lena. He instantly asked, showing anxiety in his voice, "What's the problem with Lena? I hope she is not in any kind of trouble!"

"No, Baboo! Don't get yourself worked up! Lena is a bright girl, and if she continues to work as hard as she does, she will definitely pass her examinations. But there seems to be a little problem, Baboo."

"What's the matter, Mr. Horton. If Lena is doing her work, then what is the problem?" Baboo asked with renewed anxiety.

"The matter is, Baboo, is that I have an assistant---you know his name---who is trying to court her. I am afraid that she is too young for that sort of business. It may also affect her studies."

"What should I do? Is it that Cholan guy again?" Horton nodded.

"Well," said Baboo, "if Cholan is bothering her, then why don't you tell the headmaster?" Baboo asked with surprise.

"That's the crux of the matter, Baboo! I am afraid that if I tell Mr. Hull, Mr. Cholan may be fired," Mr. Horton replied.

"Then what should I do?" asked Baboo.

"The matter has not yet gone out of hand. I already spoke to Mr. Cholan to leave Lena alone. Now, you could speak to her. Try to show her that Cholan is an ambitious and lecherous young man. Tell her not to fall for his infatuation or his sweet tongue. Tell her that boy is too pompous and that he is no good for her." Mr. Horton drank deeply into his rum and Coke. He looked at Baboo.

Baboo forgot that time was pressing. He dismissed the thought of pushing on with his tailoring. He thought of Lena. He loved all his children, but Lena gave him special joy. She was doing exceedingly well in school, and she was laying the path that his other children would follow. She was consistent with her schoolwork. She read very much.

Baboo asked, "Why would you have a repeat, teach?"

Mr. Horton positively replied. He said, "You get the drinks, Baboo. I will get the black pudding." Baboo ordered and returned to the table. After cheering each other's health with a fresh drink, Baboo said, "I will speak to her, Mr. Horton. I do not want her get tangled with a male partner as yet. She is very young, and she has much more to accomplish."

Baboo left shortly after. He did not want to be very intoxicated. He resolved to speak to Lena the following day. He felt that the matter needed his attention, and that he would talk to her on Saturday when he returned home from work.

Lena did not tell her parents of Cholan's proposal. Neither did she tell them of his impending visit. She was frightened. She felt that her father would be angry with her and would chastise for speaking to Cholan on her way home.

Baboo, on the other hand, did not get a chance to speak to Lena personally on the Saturday evening. When he arrived home, Baboo had a snack, then he took a bath. While he was bathing, Cholan had arrived. Cholan rapped on the door. Mangri peered out, then she opened it.

"Good afternoon," greeted Cholan, "I would like to speak to your husband, please."

Mangri did not know Cholan. She thought he was another customer who had come to order a pair of pants. She returned the courtesy, saying, "Presently he is in the bath. Come in and have a seat. He will be with you in a short while." Cholan entered the house and took a seat. He looked around and thought that Lena's parents were doing well for themselves.

Lena knew when Cholan had arrived. From her room, she peered through the latticed ventilation that were a few inches below the ceilings. She had climbed on the bed, then unto the middle ledge on the wall. She delicately stood on the ledge and held on to the latticed ventilation from within the room. From her vantage point, she saw Cholan entering the house. She had overheard Cholan's conversation with her mother, and her young skipped many beats.

Baboo emerged from the bathroom. Lena saw her father in his shorts and armless vests in the dining room. She thought what a handsome man her father was! Tall, slim, and very light-complexioned. His damp wavy hair was groomed backward, and as he walked in the dining room, he seemed relaxed. He was not expecting anyone. However, Mangri told him that there was someone waiting on him in the front verandah. Baboo instantly became alert. He thought, like Mangri, that it was one of his customers who had probably come for pickup.

Baboo approached the young man, scrutinized him, and realized he was a stranger. Lena climbed down from the wall and batted her ears by the cracked bedroom door.

Baboo spoke to the young man. He said, "Hi, do I know you?"

Cholan replied, not rising from his chair, "No! You do not. My name is Cholan. I am Pandit Nauth's eldest child and son. I am also a teacher at Uitvlugt Church of Scotland School."

Baboo was surprised, but he immediately became nonchalant. He extended his right hand to Cholan, who, in turn, stood up and shook hands. Baboo said, "I am very glad to meet you. Lena told me that she had a new teacher assisting Mr. Horton. She also told me that you are assisting them with evening lessons. That's very good of you,

Cholan. I am very much impressed. Now, what has brought you here this evening?"

Lena, listening, held her breath. Cholan gathered his courage and replied, "Yes, I teach Lena. I am here to tell you that I like your daughter, and I would like to marry her."

There ensued a silence. The words sank in. Baboo looked at Cholan and smiled. Baboo called Mangri, who was in the kitchen. When Mangri arrived, Baboo said, "This young man is one of Lena's teachers. He is also Pandit Nauth's eldest son and firstborn. He is here to tell us something. I will ask him to repeat what he just told me." Baboo requested of Cholan to repeat so that Mangri could hear. Cholan looked at them both and repeated.

By this time, Frank and the younger children had also entered the sitting room. Frank wanted to know what was taking his parents' attention. Frank was twelve years old when Cholan asked for the hand of Lena in marriage. It was May 1962.

Mangri was shocked, speechless! Baboo said, "Cholan, you have a very tall order. It is not easy as it seemed to you. If I am to call Lena and have her opinion, it would not have much weight because she is a minor. Furthermore, Lena is still in school, and she has her examinations. Next, I do not accept the caste system, because that was for India and not here in Guyana. However, your father is a Hindu priest as well as a businessman. Surely, he will want a Brahmin daughter-in-law. We are not Brahmins, nor are we Pandits. We are Guyanese with no affiliations to caste. Your father will not agree with your proposal, Cholan!"

Baboo took a deep breath. The few beers he had earlier loosened his tongue. He looked at the young man before him. Cholan had listened keenly to Baboo. He decided that Baboo was not an easy target. Cholan chose his words carefully when he replied, "I appreciate your views very much, Mr. Arjune. As for my father, I do not care whether he is a Pandit. None of my brothers and sisters are Pandits, nor would we follow our father and mother, who are not setting the right examples for us. All that they think about is business and receiving gifts from the poor people. Either way, they rob and cheat!"

Baboo had not expected that revelation! He felt that the young man before him was too bold, condemning his parents at the first encounter. Baboo raised his hand. "Hold it, young man! Should your father hear you, he will not appreciate what you are saying! Be aware of your reasonings, Cholan!" Baboo cautioned.

"I don't respect my parents very much," continued Cholan. "All that they do is hatch children like a hen hatches eggs! We are twelve brothers and sisters!" Cholan's face reflected anguish and disdain.

Lena, listening, did not quite well understand the trend of the conversations. She was bored.

Baboo said, "What your parents do is their concern, Cholan. But I want you to reconsider what you have told us here this evening. You are a young man, and you seem to be intelligent. I want you to go and consider carefully your proposal to us pertaining to Lena. I think that your father is also an intelligent man. By right, before you ask to marry anyone, you should at least let your parents know of your intentions. In this case, I will suggest that you discuss this matter with your parents. You should find out their views about wanting to get married to a non-Brahmin."

Cholan, angry but controlled, said, "Mr. Arjune, I am saying it finally. I do not believe in what my parents practice. I am a liberated Guyanese, and I believe, like the Arya Hindus, that anyone who is educated to read the holy scriptures is a teacher, a Pandit, or a priest. I do not believe on the old-fashioned ideas of my father that only a Brahmin can be a Pandit. What Brahmins are they? My father's entire living relatives are practicing obeah or satanic rituals!"

Baboo was shocked. This young man was a rebel! Baboo also conjectured that the young man was playing his ball in his (Baboo's) court. Baboo sensed that Cholan was probably criticizing his parents so as to influence him to consent to his marriage proposal to Lena.

Baboo queried, "Why are you so harsh on your parents? Aren't you a Hindu?"

"I don't know what I am. I cannot abide with, nor indulge in, the sickening practices of my father! I attend the Church of the Nazarene, and I sing Psalms. I find the Christian religion more simple and straightforward. My father practices a lot of mumbo jumbo!"

"Would you say that to your father? Have you ever criticized your father?" Baboo asked.

"Yes, my father knows my views. He hates me because I do not attend Hindu temples. I told him that I do not believe in exploitation," Cholan had replied.

"I think it is getting late, Cholan, and I have to work in the morning. I still recommend that you speak to your father. He should be able to advice you on your venture. I do not appreciate the idea and remember that Lena is still in school."

Cholan stood, shook Baboo's hand, and bid everyone "Good night." He departed.

The following evening, Cholan returned to Baboo's home. Baboo was off from his factory job. He was sewing at home. When Cholan knocked on the door and Baboo saw him, Baboo was annoyed. He wondered why Cholan was persisting! Baboo hid his anger and cordially invited in Cholan. He offered him a seat. He said, "Now, young man, what has brought you back so quickly? Did you speak to your parents?"

"Yes, I spoke to my dad. He said that I am a grown man and I could do whatever pleases me," Cholan replied.

"Meaning what?" asked Baboo.

"My father said that I could get married to whomsoever I chose," Cholan said.

Baboo was surprised. "Did you tell your father that the girl you love is not from a Pandit's family?"

"Yes. I explained to my parents about Lena and her parents. My father said that he knows you and that you are a decent and hardworking man. My father said he knows your relatives, in particular your elder brother, who is a member of his temple."

"Well, I still think that Lena is too young to be married. Why not pursue your career, and let's say, in about two years' time, if you are still interested, and if she loves you by that time, then the two of you could go ahead and be married."

"Two years are too long! I don't think I could wait all that while!"

"Well, give it a try. By that time, Lena will be more matured. She will finish her examinations, and she will be able to decide whether she wants to be married by then or not."

"Okay, I will wait sometime, but I promise you that I will wed no one else but Lena."

"We will wait and see," said Baboo. "Time helps to solve all problems, young man. During that time, you may meet other girls who are more educated and charming than Lena." Baboo smiled.

Cholan said seriously, "No, Mr. Arjune. Time will not make me change my mind. I will marry Lena or no one else!"

"You seemed pretty certain of yourself," said Baboo. "Let's wait and see!"

Cholan took his leave. Baboo accompanied him to the door. When Cholan was gone, Baboo slumped into a chair and spoke to Mangri. He said, "That boy seems as if he is going to be a pest. He is doing." irritates me. I don't like to be pushed, and that is exactly what Cholan is doing."

"I do not like it," said Mangri. "Those Pandit people do not like non-Brahmins marrying their children. In my lifetime, I have seen many similar marriages having serious repercussions."

"I hope that he would not pursue Lena and wreck her schooling ambitions. I have given him in which he could be aware of all circumstances that will be involved. I do hope that he will carefully reconsider," Baboo said.

He moved over to his sewing machine and resumed his work. Mangri left for the kitchen. Baboo pondered the matter as he sewed.

Chapter

4

Cholan did not adhere to Baboo's advice. Instead, he continued escorting Lena home. The neighbors began whispering. Mangri informed Baboo of Cholan's persistence.

Baboo was angry.

Two weeks later, Baboo went to see Mr. Hull, the headmaster. Baboo explained all that had transpired between Cholan and himself. Mr. Hull was very sympathetic. He promised to speak to Cholan. Mr. Hull later called Cholan in for a conference. Cholan explained that he loved Lena and that his intentions were honorable. Mr. Hull advised that he should at least let Lena finish writing her examinations. Cholan agreed.

However, as the days followed, Cholan persisted in his wooing of Lena. He disregarded Mr. Hull's advice. Baboo was worried. The neighbors were talking openly. Baboo was embarrassed. In the society, it was a shameful act for a young unmarried woman to walk the streets in the company of a particular male day after day. Baboo did not want to consent to Lena's marriage. He was adamant that she was too young! Baboo thought of reporting to the police of Cholan's harassment of his daughter. After reconsidering, he felt that that may cause more problems. Baboo talked to Lena, asking her whether she wanted to get married. He was shocked when Lena told him that she loved Cholan.

"What, you love him? Do you want to marry him?" asked Baboo, enraged.

"He continue pestering me, Daddy. He always tells me that he loves me. He asked me to marry him. Well, I will if you agree!" said Lena.

"If I agree! It's all turning back to me! If I don't agree, I will automatically become the bad person," rationalized Baboo. Baboo was puzzled. The neighbors were talking! Cholan has asked him! Now Lena loves him! Baboo reasoned, *Okay, let's wait and see.*

However, Baboo did not wait very long. Cholan visited at the end of May 1962. It was another Sunday evening. Cholan informed Baboo that he had finally decided to marry Lena. He said that he couldn't wait any longer. He told Baboo that if he did not give his consent, he would elope with Lena. That did it! Within the society, it was the most disgraceful act for one's daughter to elope. Baboo felt that he must act and do the right thing. He told Cholan, "I cannot give my consent until I have spoken to your parents. Your parents must be aware of your intentions, and I cannot take your word for it. Kindly inform your parents that I will visit them next Sunday at 4:00 p.m." Baboo was referring to the first Sunday in June.

"Okay, I will make the arrangements," agreed Cholan.

Baboo took the day off from his factory job on that date. He rested so that he would have all his faculties intact when he spoke to Pandit Nauth. Baboo and Mangri visited Pandit Nauth's residence, where the Pandit also had his store. The store was open when Baboo and Mangri stepped in. Pandit Nauth and his wife were tending to customers. Baboo waited until they had finished with the customers. Pandit Nauth looked up. He twirled the ends of his handlebar mustache with both hands, and his blue-green eyes twinkled. He looked at Baboo and Mangri and said, "What could I help you to get? We have American khaki, very thick brown cotton cloth that's good for waistbands and pockets, and we have these bales of the latest qualities in American denim."

Baboo courteously replied, "Pandit, we are not here to purchase cloth. We are here for other business, of which I am quite sure that your son Cholan had told you about!"

"My son Cholan! Business! What other business!" asked Pandit Nauth sternly. The green in his eyes sparkled. They were fiery, like a demon's.

Baboo was devastated. "You mean to say that Cholan did not tell you anything? My god! And that boy kept pestering me and making demands!" Baboo felt despair.

"What demands?" asked Pandit Nauth sternly.

"Cholan came to me and asked to marry my daughter Lena! I told him no, that she is too young. He kept pestering me. He visited me three times making the same request. Last week he said he cannot wait any longer. He wants to get married immediately. I felt that before I give him a decision, I must discuss the matter with you first," Baboo explained.

Pandit Nauth quivered with anger. He shouted, pointing at Baboo, "Don't you have any shame? Why, you are a low-caste dog! And you are here to ask for my son, a Brahmin's son, to marry your daughter!" Pandit Nauth shouted at the top of his lungs for his second son, "Sat! Sa...tt! Satesh..hh!"

Satesh, an eighteen-year-old youth, answered, "Yes, Dad! Yesss!" and came running into the store. Pandit Nauth turned toward the panting boy and screamed, "Satesh, Saat..tt run and bring me that big stick from my room. Bring it for me and let me put it on top of this f-'s head. This low-down dog has come to ask for Cholan to marry his stinking daughter! Of all the surprises in the world, this beats it! Saat! And he is not even a Brahmin! Run for that stick, Saat!"

Baboo was reeling with anger. Other customers had entered the store and were listening and looking at Pandit Nauth's exhibition. They shook their heads in disbelief. Baboo was tempted to reach over the counter and grab Pandit Nauth by the scruff of his neck. Baboo wanted to jerk the Pandit over the counter, lift him into the air bodily, and throw him onto the street. Baboo was a big man. The bedeviled Pandit was of medium height and slender built. For calling his daughter "stinking," Baboo felt that he could have pleasure of knocking the teeth out of the scrawny little man, but he controlled his anger, saying, "You should speak to your son and train him properly!

Tell him not to return by my home again!" Baboo stormed out of the store, trembling. Mangri followed behind, listening to the echo of Mrs. Nauth's swearings.

Baboo's anger mounted as he paced at home. Never in his life did he feel more insulted. It was far beyond what he had expected. He believed that Cholan had not communicated with his parents. Baboo swore that Cholan would hear from him if he ever showed up again!

Baboo sent Frank to buy refreshments. He felt that he needed to relax, that he should not allow the matter to dominate his thoughts. He felt that he needed time to resolve the issue. He knew that Pandit Nauth had behaved very irresponsibly, and that as a Hindu priest, the Pandit should have been more tolerant. Instead, he knew that Pandit Nauth had acted worse than an educated and unintelligent person.

As the evening waned, Baboo took his dinner and turned in early. He tossed about in bed until about 10:00 p.m., when there was a knock on the door. It was a dark night, and Mangri was afraid to open it. She feared that maybe there was a bandit out there!

Mangri went to get Baboo. Baboo hailed out, "Who is it?"

The person answered, "It's me, Cholan!"

Baboo was enraged anew. He felt like opening the door and punching Cholan on his nose, shattering it! Instead Baboo said, "What are you doing here now, after all the embarrassment and insults that you have caused me? You lied to me! Get out of my yard!" Baboo shouted from behind closed doors.

"Please, Mr. Arjune, let me in! Please listen to me! My father is a very jealous man and pompous. That is why he behaved in that way," Cholan pleaded in the darkness.

"Were you at home this afternoon?" harshly asked Baboo.

"No! I went for a walk on the Atlantic seawall. When I returned home, my brother, Satesh, recounted to me what my father had said," Cholan whispered with clenched jaws. "I apologize for your embarrassment, Mr. Arjune! Please let me in and listen to what I have to say."

Baboo, after his return from Cholan's parents' home, had not planned any course of action. He had gone to bed with the thought,

What will be will be. Now matters had taken a new course. Baboo opened the door, and Cholan stepped in, very humble in his disposition. Baboo offered him a seat and said, as soon as Cholan had sat, "Now let us hear what you have to say. You should have realized that you have caused enough problems already!" Mangri and the children had gathered around. The children had grown to like Cholan. They were sad when Baboo had told Lena what Pandit Nauth had said. Lena cried incessantly since. Now she was very happy to see Cholan and was anxious to hear what he had to say. She hoped and prayed that he would say the right words that will help to bring them closer together.

Cholan said, "I told my father everything and also to expect you this afternoon. My father had assured me that everything will be taken care of. I did not expect him to behave in the way he did. I am very ashamed of him, especially him being a Pandit and whatnot!"

"I have not forgiven him for his insults. I left him to fry in his own fat. I had decided to drop the entire matter and to seek a court order to restrain from pestering Lena," Baboo bluntly replied.

"Well, I intend to pester Lena for the rest of her life. I want to marry her now!" Cholan retorted sternly.

Baboo jerked backward in his chair! It was as if he was struck with a thousand volts! Mangri gaped, and Lena began shedding tears anew---tears of joy. The younger kids were jubilant. Frank was dubious. Baboo said angrily, "Cholan, this is no joking time! I am tired of all this nonsense! After all that happened today, you have the guts to return to my home and mock at me! I think I will ask you to leave in peace!

Cholan clenched his jaws. The muscles stood out, hard and knotty. Cholan piercingly replied, like a razor slicing a piece of cake, "I am not joking, Mr. Arjune. I, too, am ashamed of my father's behavior, and I want to even the score. I want to be married tonight!" Only his jaws moved. His lips quivered, as he spoke.

Baboo sensed the insistence in Cholan's voice. He couldn't figure whether Cholan was speaking with sincerity or if he was purely vengeful. Baboo said, "That's a bigger joke, Cholan. This is Sunday night, and I wouldn't rush off my daughter into a marriage like that. It is not right."

"There is no right and wrong to this, Mr. Arjune. It's love! Let's ask Lena what she thinks," suggested Cholan.

Baboo was reluctant. He did not want to drag Lena into discussion. Mangri came to the rescue. She said, "Cholan seems to be in a great rush. Wait, as Baboo suggested to you. We need have some space."

"There is no time for space," replied Cholan. "I believe in hitting the iron while it is hot! I want to get married tonight!" Cholan became more forceful as the conversation continued.

Baboo said, "It's getting late, young man. Go home and sleep. Tomorrow is another day!"

"My home is here tonight. I will sleep here after I am married. I know of this Pandit at Stewartville. His name is Sarran. He is a friend of the family. He will facilitate my marriage at any time," Cholan persisted.

Baboo condescended. He was much calmer as the night progressed. He said, "Cholan, you are dreaming. Go home now. Go and relax," Baboo coaxed.

"I will not relax until I am married tonight." Cholan looked at Lena and asked, "Lena, would you marry me?"

Lena quietly replied, "Yes."

Cholan addressed Baboo, "You heard that?" Let's cycle to Stewartville. It will only take about half an hour. Pandit Sarran usually have the relevant papers."

"Boy, I am not going anywhere tonight! You are dreaming! Marriage between Lena and you will not work out. It all started wrong. It seems as if it is not to be! What is right and what is wrong? What should be done? I don't have the answer! Go home, Cholan. Please go home!" Baboo pleaded with Cholan, hoping that time would resolve the matter.

Cholan stood up. "Okay, I am leaving. I will be back shortly!"

Baboo laughed. "You are tired, boy. Go home to bed!"

Cholan left. Baboo watched him until he was through the gate, then he shut the door to his house. He sent the children to bed and informed Mangri to awaken him at 6:00 a.m., should he fail to hear the alarm clock.

Everybody turned in and were soon asleep, except for Baboo and Mangri, who lay back in bed and reviewed the incidents of the day. Neither of them were tired. Too many things had happened in the past six hours that drove all sleep from their eyes. Their bodies ached for rest, but their minds were in turmoil. Their brains were churning, seeking the answer to this new puzzle. It was enough to contend with the neighbors and a growing family of teenagers to kindergarten ages. It was enough to cope with their work and their daily domestic chores. But they did not bargain for bombardment into forcing them to marry off their young and innocent daughter! Baboo had not foreseen problems accruing from the marriage of his children. Their firstborn, Mona, was already married, and Hanoman, their son-in-law, was treating her excellently. The young couple were progressing, and Hanoman was very supportive of Mona. Hanoman's relatives were also very nice and kind to Mona. Both Baboo and Mangri were very pleased with the marriage, and they loved Hanoman, who was a bright young man.

Baboo had not expected that Lena's life would be trespassed upon at such an early age with a proposal for marriage. He wanted Lena to be successful in school. However, he was beginning to see that there were other cogs in the wheel of Lena's life.

As Baboo talked and reminisced, he dozed and was eventually dragged into a deep sleep. But a bountiful rest was not written in his stars for the night. Shortly after he slept, Baboo was rudely awakened by a loud banging on the front door. Baboo listened and muttered, "Who the hell is it now!"

Lena shouted to her father, "Daddy, Dad, someone is rapping on the front door!"

"I heard, girl. I will go and see who it is!" Baboo looked at the bedroom clock. It was 11:45 p.m. He wondered who it was. He was not taking any chances. He picked up his nightstick and tiptoed to the door. Mangri told him to be careful. Baboo did not turn on the lights. As he approached, the rapping continued, then Baboo heard the familiar voice.

"It's me, Cholan. Sorry to bother you again. Open up please!"

Baboo instantly relaxed. However, his irritation continued. He whispered to himself, "This damn boy again! What the hell does he want now!" Aloud, Baboo said, "What is the matter now, Cholan? Didn't I tell you to go home and sleep?"

Cholan replied, "Didn't I tell you I will sleep here tonight? Now, open up. I have Pandit Sarran here with me!"

Baboo was shocked beyond comprehension. He recovered in a few seconds and said, his hands on the latches of the door, "You have to be kidding, Cholan. It is too late for any cock-and-bull story."

Pandit Sarran answered, "It is not a cock-and-bull story, Baboo. It is me, Pandit Sarran, in person, here to do service to humanity and my dear young friend, Cholan."

Baboo opened the door. Mangri had already stepped out of the room and turned on the lights when she had heard Cholan's voice. Cholan stepped in and introduced the Pandit. Pandit Sarran bowed in greeting to Baboo. Baboo returned the curtsy. Mangri also curtsied. Baboo invited them to sit down. They responded and complied, thanking Baboo.

Baboo addressed the Pandit, who was fully clothed in Indian garb. He said, "Pandit, isn't it too late for you to be out?'

"Duty calls, Baboo. Whenever humanitarian services are needed, and I could make it, I will be there to perform it. Cholan needed me, and I have answered his beckoning. Do not be surprised. Duty is duty!" Pandit Sarran spoke in his serious tone of voice. He was an elderly man, sixty-five years of age, who loved to transport himself riding his Raleigh gents sports bicycle. Pandit Sarran was tall, slim, and bespectacled. His grayed hair and mustache were very distinct against his bronzed complexion. His eyes were large and protruding and set on an angular face with a raised, pointed nose. When he smiled, his double rows of gold-capped teeth glittered like King Solomon's mine.

To Baboo's query, Pandit Sarran smiled, lighting up his face. Baboo had said, "Is this possible, Pandit? Can these young people be married at this time of night? I can't believe it!" The expression on Baboo's face was filled with disbelief.

Pandit Sarran noticed Baboo's doubt and said, "Gentlemen, I do not have the whole night to waste here. Tomorrow is a busy day for me. I have more than seven ceremonies to perform for different individuals. It will be a very tiring day for me! Now let us get on with this business so that I could at least get a couple of hours of sleep before my busy schedule begins in the morning!"

Baboo briefly studied Pandit Sarran's face. He realized that the Pandit was an astute businessman. Baboo wondered how much Sarran would receive for that night's work. Baboo made a mental note to ask later.

Pandit Sarran spoke, instantly getting down to the matter on hand. He asked, "Where is the girl?"

"She is sleeping!" replied Baboo.

"Then wake her up! How can we have a marriage without a bride?"

"Pandit, don't rush this matter!" pleaded Baboo.

"What is there to rush, Baboo? Boy likes girl, girl likes boy! They want to get married. Matter is finished! I have all the relevant documents here! They sign up, and that's it! Bang! Man and wife!" Sarran extracted a few documents form the inner pocket of his upper garment. He laid them on the table and spoke to Baboo again. "What are you waiting on? Bring the girl!"

Baboo was in a daze. His mind was blank! His brain was numb. He looked at Mangri and said, "Wake Lena. Let her tidy herself and come." Mangri obeyed.

Pandit Sarran addressed Baboo. "We are going to make this marriage right and legal. Cholan is twenty-one. That's good, and within the law. Your daughter, I learned, is fourteen years old. That is not right within the eyes of the law, if we don't have her consent before witnesses. The witnesses must be strangers. Go and wake up two of your neighbors!" Pandit Sarran ordered. "We are going to make this thing right!"

Cholan was smiling. The respected Pandit was in command. Baboo was amazed and unmoved.

Sarran, in a friendly but stern voice, said, "Go, man, go and bring us two neighbors!"

Baboo looked around. He said, "Okay, I'll go." Baboo went to his room and changed his pajamas. He dressed in casuals and put on his Wilson hat. He left, telling Mangri that he would return shortly. He walked down the street and awakened two of his acquaintances. One was a security guard at the factory, and the other was a sugarcane harvester. Baboo explained to them what was required. At first, the men protested about being awakened so late at night. They were also not very happy to be witness to a marriage ceremony at that time in the night. However, Baboo earnestly requested their services, and finally, they agreed.

Pandit Sarran was patiently awaiting Baboo's return. On entering the house, Baboo introduced the men to the Pandit and to Cholan. They remarked that they had known Cholan for quite some time. Baboo invited the witnesses to sit.

Pandit Sarran took over. He addressed Baboo's neighbors. He said, "Gentlemen, I want you to listen carefully to everything that is said here tonight. Whatever we are doing is legal, so you don't have to be afraid of breaking the law. You are merely witnesses to a marriage ceremony which I am about to perform. When the ceremony is finished and the bride and groom have signed the marriage certificates, I will request that you sign as witnesses after them. Is that clear, gentlemen?" The witnesses both answered in the affirmative.

Pandit Sarran turned to Cholan and said, "Mr. Cholan Nauth, are you willing to marry Lena Arjune, and would you oblige to sign the marriage certificates and licenses?"

Cholan clearly replied, "Yes, Pandit!"

Sarran turned to Lena. He said, "Miss Lena Arjune, are you willing to wed Mr. Cholan Nauth and to sign the marriage certificates and licenses?"

Lena also answered clearly in the affirmative.

Sarran then turned to Baboo. He asked, "Baboo Arjune, do you give your consent for your daughter, Miss Lena Arjune, who is a minor, to be married to Mr. Cholan Nauth?"

Baboo looked at Mangri. Her face was glum. Baboo turned to the Pandit. He answered, "Yes, Pandit!"

"Is there anyone present here who will object to this marriage?" Sarran finally asked. There was no reply.

"Lady and gentlemen, in your presence and in the presence of God, and with the power vested in me to be a marriage officer, I hereby pronounce Mr. Cholan Nauth and Miss Lena Arjune, as from the moment they sign the marriage licenses, to be man and wife." Pandit Sarran's voice ceased in the stillness of the night. He produced the documents and passed them on to Cholan and then to Lena, consecutively. The documents passed around the table to the two witnesses, who affixed their John Hancocks, then finally to Pandit Sarran, who examined them and uttered his satisfaction, "Very good, very good, gentlemen and now lady. I wish to offer both of you my congratulations." Pandit Sarran then uttered a few prayers in Hindi, clasping his hands and closing his eyes.

Baboo congratulated his son-in-law and gave Lena a hug. Mangri and the witnesses did the same. Pandit Sarran issued the marriage licenses, a copy each to Cholan and Lena. Lena gave hers to her father. Sarran finally said goodbye, after Cholan had promised to pay him. He took his leave.

Baboo announced that he was not reporting for work. It was already 2:00 a.m. on the Monday morning. Cholan said that he was also taking the day off. Baboo asked his neighbors if they would have a few beers to celebrate the occasion. The neighbors were reluctant, complaining that it was too early in the morning. However, at Baboo's insistence, the neighbors said, "What the hell!" They told Baboo they would also take the day off to help him celebrate! Baboo told them to give him a few minutes while he went to wake up the shopkeeper to get some supplies.

Cholan offered to accompany his father-in-law. Together they went to the grocery store and awakened the owner. They purchased a case of Banks beers, soda, ice cubes, canned meats, snacks, and confectionaries. On arrival home, Baboo offered the beers to his neighbors and to Cholan. Mangri, Lena, and Frank helped themselves to snacks and soda. The other children were asleep.

The men drank their beers and engaged in mutual discussions of current events in the country until it was break of day. The neighbors, feeling much happy, left for their homes by 6:00 a.m. Baboo announced that he would turn in to get a few hours' sleep. Before leaving, Baboo instructed Mangri to show Cholan to a room where he could rest.

As Baboo was leaving, Cholan said, "This evening I am taking Lena over to my parents' home."

Baboo turned abruptly and replied, "That would be good. I don't think that I could object, because you are married, but your parents may not take it lightly!"

"That's why I am taking her over. I want to surprise them. I want them to be shocked," said Cholan.

"Then do as you will," said Baboo. He then turned to Mangri and said, "See that he packs her best clothing and let her take her jewelry---chain, bracelets, earrings, everything that she has."

"I will do my best," Mangri said in a daze. Mangri couldn't believe that it was happening. Only a year before, Mona was married, and she left the home with her husband. Now, suddenly, her second child was leaving. There was no warning! There was no preparation! Mangri felt that a void was being created in her home and in her life. She felt that her daughters were leaving her, deserting her, that they have not spent adequate time of their teenage lives with her! She looked upon Lena as a baby, a baby that was married, and for what? To bring more babies in this world!

Baboo, on the other hand, had been thinking further afield. He felt that circumstances surrounding Lena's marriage were all strange. Things had happened too quickly, as if the pieces were all made and were falling into their places. He felt that he had not any control on the situation. Cholan was leading him on all the while. On the night of the marriage, he had felt like an invalid, as the scenes were being acted before his very eyes. He had felt like a coerced player who could not have extricated himself from the web that was being woven around him by the actors on the stage.

Baboo hoped that the marriage would work. He wished Lena and Cholan well of their loves together. He hoped all the best for Lena and her husband.

Chapter

5

Outwardly, Cholan's parents had not rejected Lena completely. Nor had they welcomed her with open arms. Her father-in-law, Pandit Nauth, literally ignored her. Her mother-in-law showed some measure of politeness and spoke to her from time to time. Cholan's younger brothers and sisters took to her from the very beginning. His elder brothers and sisters saw Lena as a playmate who could be manipulated at their whims and fancies.

Lena's first day of marriage life was her last day at school. As it was the rule in the society, no married or pregnant child was allowed to attend the community schools. Lena became a housewife and a domiciled worker in the home of her in-laws. She was trained by her mother-in-law to cook the meals, clean the house, and do the laundry for the large family. She worked from dawn to beyond dusk. In the mornings, she made breakfast for them all, then packed lunches for the children to take to school. She prepared the lunches of her mother and father-in-laws, who worked at home in their store. At dinnertime, she cooked for the entire family.

Cholan did not attempt to send Lena to attend private classes, nor did he teach her any longer. It was a strange life that she led in the household of strangers and a complete turnaround from her life of school, friendliness, and leisure at home.

Overnight, Lena became a young woman with an overdose of responsibilities. Cholan had thought that for his parents to accept his wife, Lena would have had to serve them well. On the other hand, Lena did not know better. She felt that her husband was right to ask her to do whatever he wished of her. For Lena, Cholan was always right. After all, he was a teacher! She felt that he knew best! Cholan, at the same time, tried, through his young wife's work, to win the favor of his parents. At no time did he consider Lena's situation, other than that of helping in the house.

Whenever, Lena brought up the subject of furthering her education, Cholan would reply, "Later. There is always time for that." In September 1962, Cholan was accepted at the In-service Teacher's Training College in Georgetown. It involved working during the day and attending classes at nights. It was a three-year program at the College, and it entailed Cholan spending his nights in Georgetown. There was no ferry across the Demerara River after 8:00 p.m.

Lena worked like a horse during the day and slept alone at nights, except on weekends, when Cholan would sometimes be at home. During the weekdays, Lena only saw Cholan briefly during the mornings when he dropped in at home for a rushed breakfast.

Baboo, on the other hand, tried to keep his family together. Frequently, on weekends, Baboo would invite his daughters and sons-in-law to family get-togethers. At one of these family get-togethers, both Mona and Lena announced that they were pregnant. Baboo and his family were overjoyed.

On that evening, as the ladies prepared dinner, Baboo and his sons-in-law drank beers. As Cholan became intoxicated, he told Hanoman that Lena would get a son. He boasted, "My wife will get a boy, and he will be a doctor when he grows up."

"Come off it, Cholan! I wish your child all the best," replied Hanoman, "but first you must pray that she gets a safe delivery and that both the baby and the mother will be well," continued Hanoman.

"What! Are you saying that my wife is not healthy?" persisted Cholan.

"No! I am merely saying that whatever the sex of my child is when it is born doesn't matter to me now. All that I hope and wish is for her to give birth safely and that both baby and mother will be well!"

"Well spoken!" said Baboo. "That is the way that both of you should think."

"Are you taking his side?" asked Cholan angrily.

"No! I am not taking anyone's side! I am merely agreeing with the same thing that you should do now. Let's face facts, Hanoman is right! Both my daughters' health is involved!" Baboo emphasized. He continued, "The main idea now is for them to join maternity clinics and have regular physicals."

Cholan said, "I am sorry, but my wife doesn't have the time to go to clinics. She has enough to do at home as it is."

Baboo was infuriated, but he held his calm. Several times Lena had visited since her marriage, and Baboo had noticed marks of violence on Lena's face and arms and other parts of her body. Baboo had questioned Mangri whether Lena had complained of ill-treatment. Mangri had told him that Lena only cried whenever she was asked about the bruises.

That evening, when Cholan and Hanoman met at Baboo's home, Hanoman had observed Lena's marks of violence. Cholan's reply that his wife cannot join a maternity clinic angered Hanoman to such an extent that Hanoman openly accused Cholan, "You seem to be very inhumane. For one, you will be jeopardizing the lives of Lena and the baby if she doesn't join a maternity clinic, and two, I have seen bruises and blue-black blotches on her face and under her eyes. I believe that you are beating that girl!"

Cholan was angered beyond his control. He blurted, "Mind your damn business, and watch your own wife. Aren't you satisfied that you have one sister? Now you want both! I knew you were envious of me because you can't even match my qualifications!"

"I don't want any quarrels between you two guys. I don' want any quarrels in my house. If you boys can't drink a few beers and talk sensibly, then let's quit now!" Baboo was stern in his admonition.

"I am not going to stop," said Cholan, "This damn backward fool here is going to tell me how to run my life! Why don't he go back to school as I am doing, to be somebody! All he does is to pass trains!"

"Shut up!" shouted Baboo, "I said no more of that!"

Mona and Lena heard their father shouting. They came into the sitting room with their mother. Mona went to Hanoman and whispered in his ears. Hanoman told her to relax, that he was in control of himself. Lena went to Cholan and asked him to accompany her to the kitchen.

Instead of calming himself or granting Lena her request, Cholan stood up and slapped Lena across the face, screaming, "Don't tell me what to do! Never tell me what to do again!" He punched her in the face. Lena's lips split, and the blood gushed down the front of her dress. Then all hell broke loose.

Tall, handsome, austere Baboo climbed to his full height, of the six-footer that he was, and packed his left and right ambidextrous fists into Cholan's face. In quick succession, the fists made contact with flesh and bones, as Cholan was beaten backward to the floor!

Enraged, Baboo muttered, as his fists packed the punches, "I knew that you were beating her a long time now...your neighbors told me...but of all the evil, your greatest is to strike my daughter before my eyes in my own home! I tolerated you, hoping for the best, but you don't seem to be doing right by my daughter!" Baboo, in his pent-up anger, wanted to finish him off, but Hanoman, Mona, and Mangri flung themselves upon Baboo, trying to get him away from the cowering Cholan.

Frank shouted at his father, "Daddy, leave him alone! Daddy!"

Baboo looked up and saw the eyes of his infuriated son. The eyes met in electrifying glare. Within a split second, Baboo received Frank's message, and he held back the finishing touches, on Cholan. Baboo shook like a wounded giant and sat down.

Hanoman and Lena tried to render first aid to Cholan. Cholan shoved Hanoman away. Lena helped him to his feet. Cholan croaked to her, "Let's go home! Let's get out of here!"

Baboo overheard and told Lena "Don't go, Lena! If you say the word, we will end this marriage now! You could get a divorce on the ground of brutality, Lena! Don't go with him."

Lena looked at her father and cried. She said, "Daddy, he had this coming to him a long time now. I tried to hide it from you, but I didn't know that you knew." She sobbed, "Daddy, that has been going on for a year now, but I didn't complain. I always tell Ma that all is well, but from the very first week we were married, he has been beating me." She cried loudly, letting out all the sorrow she had tied within her chest. All eyes were upon her. Cholan sobered up, staggered to the door. He screamed, "Lena! Let's go!"

Lena stood immobile, hysterical. Mona went to her and tried to comfort her. Mangri went to her and hugged her in her arms. But Lena let it all out, "Daddy, he calls me a dunce, but he doesn't want me to go to school! He calls me backwards, but it is him who caused me to leave school! He often beat me in front of his parents to please them." She sobbed and dabbed at her eyes.

Baboo repeated, "Lena, do not return with him! I am begging you, don't go back!"

"Daddy, he is my husband. I have made my bed, and I have to lie in it! Daddy, I will go. Even if he kills me, I will go. I have already caused you enough problems, Daddy. I do not want to bring my problems to you anymore." Lena sobbed, her tears streaming down her face.

"Lena, you are not causing me problems. I could deal with them. I will take care of you and the baby. You are not a burden. You will never be a burden for me!"

"Daddy, I have learnt Hindi. I have read the Ramayan! Where Rama went, Sita followed!"

"He is not Rama! Don't follow him, Lena," pleaded Baboo.

"Daddy, I must go!" She ran out of the house and into the yard. Cholan followed her downstairs. At the fountain, in Baboo's yard, Cholan washed his battered face. Lena helped him. Cholan took off his shirt. Lena took one of her father's shirt that was hanging on the clothesline to dry and helped Cholan into it. Together they walked out of her father's yard. Mona, Hanoman, Mangri, Baboo, and the children watched them go. The children were crying. Frank tried to pacify the kids, telling them, "Shh, shh, she will be okay. Don't worry. If he beats her, Daddy will get him!"

Shortly after that incident, Cholan and Lena moved out of Cholan's parents' home. Cholan rented a house on the East Coast of Demerara, at Lilendaal. Cholan transferred to a school at Industry, not far from the house he had rented. He brought home a friend and introduced her to Lena. She was beautiful, shapely, and three years Lena's senior. She was a Pearl in name and nature and was an assistant teacher at the Industry Primary School.

When Lena was in her seventh month of pregnancy, Cholan's absence from home became more regular. Cholan had moved to the east coast so as to have easy access to his college, home, and job. College was now separated from his job by a distance of about five miles and half an hour by taxi. However, since his friendship with Pearl, Cholan started to cut college classes on some evenings. Sometimes, on weekends, he told Lena that he had to go to the library, but he never did! Instead, he dated Pearl. They were regular visitors to the Carib Hotel on the east coast of Demerara.

Lena knew that Cholan was having an affair. Through her woman's instincts and intuition, she found various evidences on Cholan's clothing. His shirts would have blotches of lipstick, which he never tried to hide, his shirts and vests smelled of women's perfume, his undershorts smelled of female body fluids, and sometimes there were long dark hairs on his clothing.

At first, when Lena found the evidence, she would question Cholan. These sessions would end up in arguments. Once, Cholan slashed Lena on her neck with a kitchen knife.

When she scented the female body fluids on his shorts, which he had probably used to wipe himself, she had confronted him with the evidence. He was so furious that he had beaten her into a temporary state of coma. When she came to herself, regaining consciousness, she found herself lying on the cold greenheart floor of the house, and her swollen abdomen was bandaged. Cholan was not in sight. She peered around, then opened the bloodied bandages. What she saw made her lose consciousness again for a few minutes. When she came to, blinded with tears and hysteria, she replaced the bandages on the six inches of knife slice at the right side of her stomach. She crawled to the bed and shook like a leaf, with fear. She felt that she would lose the baby, but as the evening wore on and nothing happened, she realized that the wound was not deep enough to dislodge the baby.

She had wanted to crawl out of the house and go to the closest neighbor for help, but on second thoughts, she said to herself, *Death comes when it comes.* She slept fitfully.

Cholan came in the house after midnight. He asked her, when he shook her awake, "Do you want a cup of tea?" She started to tremble. He felt her shivering under the covers. He quickly went to the kitchen and made her a warm cup of tea. He lifted her head and literally forced the tea down her throat. He then removed the covers and uttered the greatest surprise in the world, "My god! What is the problem with you? What did you try to do to yourself? He peeled the cover further back and loosened the bandages. "Oh no! You tried to kill yourself and the baby! I have to report this to the police!" Lena became hysterical again. Her sobbing became ceaseless. "You are crying to get my sympathy! No! You tried to harm yourself and to kill my baby! I am going to get you locked up!" Lena fainted.

When she came to, Cholan had a cold compress on her forehead. He said, "All right, I am not going to report the matter to the police. I do not want you to go to the doctor. If you do that, I will report you. I will take care of this wound myself, as I did while you fainted." She looked down at herself. She had fresh bandages, and they were not stained with blood. Later that night, she slept. She did not go to the doctor.

By the month of May, 1964, Cholan dropped out of college. He took a transfer to Zeeburg Secondary on the west coast of Demerara. His parents acquired a house at Zeeburg public road, and Cholan and Lena moved their residences into new quarters.

Cholan revisited his father-in-law's home, pretending as if nothing had happened. Lena, secretly told her mother that all was going well and that the baby was due in June.

Mangri asked, "Have you joined any maternity clinic?"

"No!" replied Lena. "I planned to get the baby at home."

"But you are still very young, and this is your first child! You should give birth at a hospital!" Mangri said worriedly.

"No, Ma! I've decided to give birth at home when the time comes."

"Okay. In that case, when you are close, you would come home here. We have one of the best midwives in the village. I will speak to her. I will also speak to the washer woman. Don't be afraid! I will make all the arrangements! I am very happy that you have returned to live nearby," Mangri told her.

"Thanks, Ma! I will be very happy to come home. You make me feel very comfortable, Ma." Lena smiled.

"That reminds me," Mangri said, "did anyone ever speak to you about what to expect when your time has come to give birth?"

"No, Ma! I gathered a little information by reading. That's all book knowledge!

"Well, girl, listen...." They were in the kitchen. Mangri told her all she needed to know about birthing.

In the meantime, Cholan was sitting in the front verandah, opposite his father-in-law as he sewed on the machine. They were hitting it off in a friendly tone. Baboo was careful to avoid asking anything that would get under Cholan's skin.

Cholan told him, "My father bought a huge water vat that is lying in the yard. He will be very happy if you could set it up so that we could get water in the house."

Baboo smiled happily. He wanted to make amends. He wanted Lena to have a happy life. He said, "That's easy work. I will gladly set it up for your father. Let's say, in the next two weeks' time. I will be due for my one-week annual leave. I will do it then, if that will be to your father's convenience!"

"That will do fine! I will tell my father," Cholan replied.

In fact, the truth was, that Baboo had planned to complete his tailoring contracts during his annual leave. However, he felt that if the sacrifice would compensate for Lena's happiness, then it was worth the while.

Baboo and Frank worked on setting up the water vat. They completed the job in four days' time, at the end of which Cholan and Lena had water leading to their kitchen and bathroom in the house. At no time during the work period did Pandit Nauth show up, even to give moral support. Cholan, of course, made excuses that his father was out performing religious rites for people in the villages.

When Lena's time was close for delivery, she moved to her parents' home at the beginning of June 1964. At that time, Guyana was undergoing a political crisis, and the country was on the verge of a civil war. The British troops were brought into the country to maintain law and order.

Cholan did not visit Lena during her final days of pregnancy. Lena yearned to see him, but he did not show up. She sent Frank to the house at Zeeburg with messages to Cholan, but the messages were undelivered. Cholan was not there.

Lena gave birth on June 16, at 5:00 p.m. Baboo went for the midwife when Lena had started with her labor pains. The midwife, a trained registered nurse, was very skillful, and Lena birthed with no unusual labor problems. It was a bouncing baby girl, who, from the inception of birth, screamed her way into the world.

Late that night of June 16, 1964, Baboo received messages that his son-in-law, Cholan Nauth, was arrested and was in police custody. The cop told Baboo that Cholan was charged with attempted murder. Baboo and Mangri withheld the information from Lena, for fear that she may be shocked, and that may enhance hemorrhage. Both Lena and the baby were doing fine. Baboo wanted them to continue being that way.

At about that period of time, in 1964, Baboo had enclosed the bottom of his house, around the concrete stilts. He had used first-quality greenheart and mora lumber to do the construction. His handiwork resulted in the creation of a beautiful apartment.

Baboo had specifically built his apartment for Hanoman and Mona, because Hanoman had been transferred to a railway station at Vergenoegen, not very distant from Baboo's village. Baboo had also wanted to help the young couple by saving them the burden of paying house rent. At the time of Lena's delivery, Mona and Hanoman had already move into their new apartment at Baboo's residence.

On the evening of June 16, when Baboo had received the messaged of Cholan's arrest and charge, Baboo waited until Hanoman had returned home from work. Later that evening, Baboo and Hanoman cycled to the police precinct to see Cholan. Cholan cried when he saw his visitors. He told them that he had not known why or how he did what he did.

Baboo and Hanoman learnt that Cholan had chopped his maternal grandfather several times on the neck and shoulders. Cholan had used a cutlass in the brutal attack, and the seventy-five-year-old man had bled profusely and was in a coma. Cholan was told, at the time of his arrest, that should the old man die, he would be charged with murder.

The incident occurred when Cholan had overheard his mother and his grandfather quarrelling over the distribution of the old man's properties. Cholan's mother was accusing her father for giving shares to his sons who were not residing with them, in the same yard that Cholan's father had his home and his shop.

Mrs. Nauth told her father that he had no right to pass on properties to his sons, who were already rich and were the owners of many properties themselves. She argued that she did not want her brothers to live on the same estate with her immediate family. The old man had insisted that it would be better for her family unity if they all lived together. Mrs. Nauth was not in agreement. She shouted at her father and accused him for favoring his sons. The old man threatened to disinherit her. Cholan had overheard, and became angry at his grandfather's threat.

Cholan grabbed a cutlass and attacked the old man. He dealt him several chops, then he dopped the cutlass and ran. His mother had screamed and ran out of the house as the old man fell and lay bleeding on the floor. The police were called in by neighbors. They combed the neighborhood and arrested Cholan on the seawall. Cholan was contemplating suicide by drowning. The cops had reached him on the nick of time to make the arrest.

The old man did not die. After four days in jail, Cholan was released. Bail was posted by his mother. On his release, Cholan visited his wife and infant child. They named her Enrika, after her mother, Lena.

In the latter half of June, Mona also gave birth to her first child. He was a handsome baby boy. They named him after his father, Hanoman Singh Jr. Baboo's home was loud with joy and baby screams. Everyone was busy doing things for the babies and their mothers. The house was transformed into a hive of activities. Cholan visited more often. Whenever he came, a pall of gloom hung around him. Everyone was perturbed with the charge he faced. His job hung in the balance. Should he be convicted, he would lose his job as a teacher.

Because the babies had arrived so close together, Baboo and Mangri decided to have a joint celebration in honor of the two youngsters. All delicious foods were prepared, and the family met in calm and merriment. Baboo had opened a bottle of Scotch whiskey to commemorate the occasion. They were friendly discussions around the table. Cholan thought of his own problems and condescended to discussions.

Hanoman had challenged, "How is baby Enrika doing, Cholan? She is a beautiful child! You didn't get as you had predicted!"

"Don't hold me to that!" replied Cholan. I was much younger and stupid then. Too many things have happened since, and when I reflected on them, they make me regret!"

"I hope that you have really grown up! You are now a man of additional responsibilities, and your family do need you!" Hanoman advised.

"How is the case coming up, Cholan? Do you think that will get off? If you don't want to speak about it, I will understand!" Baboo was probing, and at the same time, he was very cautious, looking for any adverse reactions from Cholan. Baboo did not trust Cholan, since the last incident involving his grandparent.

"I hope that it will wash out," said Cholan. "My mom is working on her father to drop the matter. So far, the old man has not consented," replied Cholan.

"And how is he?" asked Baboo. "Have all his wounds been healed?"

"He is mending well. Every time I look at the old coot, I regret the incident. He is making all attempts to avoid me!" Cholan said with regret.

"Does he communicate with your mom and your siblings?" asked Baboo.

"Yes! That is what eats me up. We live in the same yard, we pass each other every day, but the old boy just sees through me!"

"It is too bad, Cholan. You have been extremely wrong to your grandfather. The crime is unforgivable! I hope for the sakes of my daughter and granddaughter, that the old man decides to save your soul!" Baboo said, with much concern in his voice.

They sipped their whiskey and soda. They chewed on their roasted pork. Cholan relished the well-seasoned garlic roasted pork.

"Let bygones be bygones and let's hope for the best for you guys and your families in the future. Congratulations to both of you on your newborns," Baboo said. They filled their glasses. Hanoman said, lifting his glass, "To us and our families." They echoed, "To us!" and drank.

Cholan's grandfather did not appear in court to lead evidence against Cholan. The magistrate, at the preliminary inquiry, threw out the case for lack of evidence. Cholan was warned by the magistrate and released.

6

In September 1964, Cholan registered at the University of Guyana for his bachelor of arts degree, majoring in Spanish.

Lena was pregnant with her second child. She was very occupied with taking care of Enrika and her household chores. Cholan taught at Zeeburg Secondary School during the day and attended the University in Georgetown at nights. Cholan had easy access to meals because his home and school were in the same village. When he arrived home in the mornings Lena would have his breakfast ready on the table. She waited on him. After breakfast, it took him ten minutes to walk to work. At lunchtime, Cholan would walk home to a meal that was warm and ready. Lena was always there for him!

In the evenings, when school was dismissed, Cholan would walk across to get his books and an evening snack. Lena would have his dinner packed and ready in his shoulder bag. Cholan had it made! Lena waited on him at all times and tried her best to please him.

Sometimes when Lena finished her chores at home and Enrika was asleep, Lena felt lonely and bored. She read as much as she could, but she was tired with Mills and Boons and Barbara Cartland. Lena wanted something more challenging to do. From a neighbor she borrowed an old typewriter and a Pitman's shorthand book. Lena started practicing on the typewriter and reading and writing shorthand.

By the time Cholan found out of Lena's venture, she had almost mastered keyboard. She used to hide the old worn-out typewriter under the bed. She knew that Cholan was jealous of her and would not appreciate it if she learned to type. She had proposed to him to let her attend typing classes in her parents' village, but he disagreed at all times, using Enrika as an excuse. Lena had argued that Mangri was prepared to babysit Enrika while she went to the classes in the evenings. Cholan had told her he would not allow anyone to take care of his daughter.

Cholan found the typewriter under the bed one Sunday morning when he was searching for a book he had misplaced. "Lena!" he shouted. "Whose typewriter is this?'

Lena was preparing breakfast. She ran into the room. She feared that something had happened to Enrika. When she entered the room, she saw Cholan had the typewriter in his hands. She looked at his face, and the blood drained from her heart in fear. Cholan's eyes looked wild and devil-like.

"Whose typewriter is this?" Cholan hissed.

"I borrowed it from the neighbor!" Lena said meekly.

"Why did you borrow it?" he screeched.

"I am learning to type!"

"Didn't I tell you not to learn to type? You think you are going to do as you like?" Cholan lurched forward and flung the typewriter at Lena. It struck her with a tremendous impact on her chest. She fell backward and lost consciousness. How long she was blacked out, she did not remember, but when she came to, she found herself lying on the floor, and Enrika was asleep on her stomach.

Lena awoke with much pain about her body. Her chest and head ached. Her head was throbbing. She gently felt the back of her head, and to her surprise, there was a large bump. She had struck her head when she fell on the hard greenheart floor. She gently eased Enrika from her chest and on to the floor. Enrika slept soundly. With much effort and pain, Lena dizzily got to her feet. She held on to the wall for support. Groggily, she walked to the bed and lay down for a while. Cholan was not in the house.

Lena thought of what she should do. As she breathed, her chest pounded with pain. Crying, she slowly got up and tried to pack a shoulder bag with a few pieces of Enrika's clothing. She staggered into the kitchen and gathered Enrika's food and nursing bottle. She placed those items into the shoulder bag. Gradually her mind began to clear. She rinsed her face and straightened her hair. She picked up the sleeping Enrika in her arms and then slung the shoulder bag on her right shoulder. She stepped out of the house and locked the door. She caught a taxi and went to her parents' house.

Baboo was reading the *Sunday Chronicle* newspapers when Lena arrived. Baboo was in relaxing mood, but at the sight of Lena, he became very disturbed. He knew instantly that something was wrong. He asked, "What is the matter, Lena? You seem to be in much pain."

Mangri approached her and took Enrika. Lena placed the shoulder bag on the floor. She cried, streams of tears running down her cheeks. Mangri led her to a seat and gave her a towel to wipe her eyes. Enrika was laid to sleep on the sofa.

Crying, Lena recounted to her parents what had happened. Baboo became angry. He asked, "Did he do that and he knows that you are pregnant?" Baboo became indignant. "Cholan is a heartless son of a bitch. He could have killed you! I am surprised you didn't lose the baby immediately. That boy is crazy, or something serious is wrong with his brains!"

Lena continued sobbing.

Baboo said, "I will advise that you remain here as long as you want. If he comes here, that will be another problem. But you stay and take care of your child. In the meantime, you could go to commercial classes!"

Lena said, "Daddy, I am not scared of him. Very easily he becomes violent. He beats me up for the least error. I don't know what to do!" She started crying in another torrent of tears.

Enrika awoke and called in her baby talk for her mommy. Lena went to her. She took out the baby food from her bag and fed Enrika.

Baboo said, "I am tired with your unfortunate situation. There seemed to be no change in Cholan. Instead of improving and have a happy family life, he's getting worse day by day!"

Baboo decided not to get worked up. He realized that he had a family to care for, and it was not worth it to go to jail for Cholan. Baboo decided to play a wait-and-see game.

Cholan did not inquire of Lena and Enrika for the next month. Neither did he visit. By the end of 1964, Lena learnt that Cholan was seeing another woman. Christmas passed, and Lena did not receive any card from her husband. There were no gifts nor financial support for Enrika from her father.

Lena, however, attended her business classes and was successful at her Pitman's examination in typewriting and shorthand. She gave birth at her parents' home to a bouncing baby boy in 1965. She named her son Devo, after a famous Indian film star.

After the birth of Devo, Lena began receiving letters from Cholan. In these letters, he lavished her with his eternal love. Gradually Cholan began waiting to see her at street corner where he knew she would pass. Cholan followed her on his cycle, wooing her love all over again. Cholan reminded her of the Ramayan, that Sita never deserted her Rama.

Lena, for want of better judgment, fell for Cholan's honey savored words and endearments. She announced to her parents that she would be returning to her husband. Mangri was reluctant to let her go. Mangri told her, "Why listen to the sweet words of that boy, Lena? He is only fooling you. He will treat you the same way, like dirt, when you return. All that he will do is get you pregnant then kick you out again!"

"Ma, he is my husband! I have to go back to him! I have two children, and they have to be fed!"

"Aren't they eating? Aren't you eating?"

"Yes, Ma! But I cannot burden you with my problems for the rest of my life!"

"You are not a burden to us, Lena! We love your children! Your father is not complaining either. He wants you to remain!"

"Ma, I know that the right thing for me to do is to return to my husband!"

Mangri gave up. She knew that she couldn't convince Lena. Baboo, on the other hand, told her that she was big enough to make her own decision. "Whatever you decide, to do Lena, is okay with me," her father had told her.

When Devo was two months old, Lena left with her two children to live with Cholan at his parents' home in Uitvlugt. The Pandit and his wife continued to ignore Lena. However, they loved their grandchildren. In their hypocrisy, they accepted the grandchildren as Brahmins. They did not acknowledge that their grandchildren's mother was a human being like themselves.

When Pandit Nauth saw his grandson for the first time, he held him in his hands and read verses from the Ramayan and the Geeta, then he blew on his grandson, blessing him. Pandit Nauth had said to his wife, "My dear, we have a new Brahmin in our family. Cholan has given us a fine grandson!"

Mrs. Nauth had replied, "Yes, dear. He will be just like his grandfather, picking up in his grandfather's footsteps!"

Mangri and Baboo, who had endeared themselves to Lena's children, were very sad when she left with them. Enrika had become Mangri's joy, and Devo was her little angel for the two months she had cared for him. Mangri and Baboo accepted that they had no control on their grandchildren's lives and that they could only pray for their well-being.

Lena's lot was not changed from the first time she had lived with her in-laws. She continued to be given the domestic chores as well as caring for her two children. Cholan did not pay her much attention, and her in-laws ignored her. Lena took solace in tending to her children and watching them grow.

Cholan was successful at his first year's examinations at the university. During his second year, Cholan rented an apartment in Georgetown. He hired a young woman from Georgetown to do his cleaning and to prepare his dinner. In time, Cholan befriended the young lady. He invited her to move in to his apartment so that she could better care for him and to avoid wasting time to travel to her part-time job there. Not very long after the young lady moved into Cholan's apartment, she became his live-in mistress.

Cholan began to miss classes during his second year at the university. His professors had warned him that he had qualified with his attendance to pass his courses. Cholan dropped out from the university as a result. Cholan did not tell Lena that he had dropped out of the university. Instead, after his work on the west coast during the daytime, Cholan traveled as usual to Georgetown in the evenings. He spent the time enhancing his relationship with his lover. On many weekends, Cholan did not return home to Lena and the children. Whenever Lena asked him where he was, he would beat her.

Lena remained with her children, in sorrow, at her in-laws' home. She devoted her time and effort to care for Enrika and Devo, her two beautiful and loving children. Lena tried to be the obedient wife and to take care of Cholan's needs whenever he showed up at home. Cholan, on the other hand, in order to be closer to his mistress and to devote as much time to her as possible, transferred as a teacher to the Guyana Oriental College in Georgetown, and there he remained until 1967, teaching and living a life of promiscuity and desertion from his family.

Several times during these years Lena contemplated suicide, but the smiling faces of her darling children always stopped her from committing suicide. Lena also gained courage by constantly looking out for her father, who passed her way to and from work. The mere glimpse of Baboo gave her inspiration to live on. She did not burden her parents with her woes, nor was she allowed to visit her parents to communicate. Her in-laws kept her in the house with threats that should she leave, she would not be allowed to return and her children would be taken away from her. Lena feared losing her children. She did not visit her parents, nor did she think of communicating with them through letters. She totally succumbed to the guiles of her in laws.

Chapter

7

In 1967, Lena's brother, Frank, having been successful at the London General Certificate in Education, Ordinary Levels, was appointed as a pupil teacher at the Leonora Primary School.

Baboo had accompanied his son to meet the headmaster of the school. Mr. Moses, the headmaster, was very pleased with Frank's qualifications and had decided to help the young man. Mr. Moses followed through in the appointment of Frank, who started working as a young teacher on April 27, 1967. Frank was 17 years old.

Baboo was very proud of Frank. He boasted to his friends, in friendly chatter, that his son was a teacher. He further told them that Frank was planning to attend the university to do his bachelor's degree. Baboo lavishly celebrated his son's appointment with his friends. He was joyous and happy.

Baboo also felt that Lena had settled down. He was not receiving any news from her, and he felt that no news was good news. Baboo's eldest daughter, Mona, by 1967, had also given birth to her third child, a daughter. Baboo and Mangri were very proud of their grandchildren from Mona and Hanoman. The kids---Hanoman Jr., Latchman, and Rohini---were all healthy and adoring children. Baboo and Mangri loved them, and missed Lena's at the same time.

Frank had ridden on his bicycle on his way from work on December 12, 1967. The sun was scorching hot, and Frank sweated profusely on his arrival home. He took off his soaked shirt and sat in the shade of the front stairway of his parents' house. Frank was beginning to cool off from the Atlantic trades that were blowing across the coastland, when his mother brought him the mail. Frank looked at the mail and realized that it was very important. The sender's name and address were: The registrar, Victoria Law Court, Brickdam, Georgetown. The mail was addressed to Baboo Arjune.Frank looked at the envelope and wondered why the supreme courts had written his father. He reflected on the events over the last year and concluded that Baboo had not been involved in any wrongdoing. At that time, Frank knew, the neighbors were very cantankerous, but Baboo was ignoring them. Baboo was not charged with any offense.

Frank told his mother that the mail had arrived from the courts in Georgetown. Mangri became very worried and told Frank to open it. Frank had replied, "It is for Father, Mom. I do not want to open it! I do not want to pry in his business!"

Mangri had replied, "It is a very important court letter. Your father will not be angry if you open it. I don't want him to be shocked when he reads it. So now, open it!"

"I still don't want to open it, Mom. It is not my mail," protested Frank.

"Give me that letter," said Mangri. Frank passed the letter. Mangri took it and opened the envelope. She took out the folded sheet of paper and stretched out her hand to Frank. "Here, read it!"

Frank reluctantly took the letter, unfolded it, and read to himself. He couldn't believe what he saw. He reread a second time. Mangri was impatient. "What is it, boy?" she asked. "Read it aloud!" she commanded.

Frank read it to her and explained. Lena was divorced. It was the court's order that annulled her marriage to Cholan. It stated that since she had failed to appear in court to contest Cholan's petition for a divorce, the court had granted him his petition in her absence.

Frank was appalled. Mangri was experiencing severe shocks. She became doubtful. She kept repeating, "It can't be! It can't be! Lena is still with that dog, and she is living at his parents' home! She was there all the time! It can't be true!"

Frank somberly said, "Ma, it is true. This is an official document from the Supreme Court of Guyana. Why it was sent to Dad, I do not know. Lena is divorced, Ma. It is true." Frank pointed to the document. "Here, Ma, is the official seal of the court. This is not a tampered document. It is a fact!"

"How could it be, when she is still living with her husband and children?" asked Mangri.

"It beats me, Ma. I don't understand! But it is true."

As Frank and Mangri debated the matter, Baboo arrived home with a huge parcel on the handlebar of his bicycle.

Frank assisted him to take the parcel upstairs. When they had set it down on the floor, Baboo excitedly said, "I have great news! The personnel manager of the sugar plantation awarded me the contract today to sew new uniforms for all the security guards of the estate. After work this afternoon, I stopped in at the store and bought four bolts of the best American khaki. I will make about fifty percent profit from this job." Baboo was jubilant. He jumped up, clapped his hands, and let off an Indian war whoop.

Frank smiled. Mangri did not join her husband in his hilarity. Baboo noticed her silence and asked, "What is the matter? What happened today? It is the neighbors again?" Baboo had expected her to complain about the neighbors cursing her or threatening to beat her.

Mangri did not answer his question. She walked over to him and silently handed him the letter. He read. He instantly sat down. He quietly said, "Frank, read this letter aloud to me, please." Frank read aloud. Baboo took off his safety helmet and flung it on the floor. He angrily shouted, "It can't happen! That is wrong! She is living with that son-of-a-bitch right now! It can't be!" Baboo was indignant.

"It is true, Daddy. This is an official letter. Here is the seal of the court!"

Baboo looked at the seal and shook his head in disbelief.

"It can't be!" he repeated. "Only this morning, I saw her on my way to work! She is still there in her matrimonial home with her two children!"

"What do you think we should do daddy?" asked Frank.

"We have to go and tell her. We have to get her out of there! According to this, she is no longer his wife! She has no right there anymore," Baboo reasoned.

"But, Daddy, there are many of them living there. Maybe they all know about this. Maybe Pandit Nauth and his entire family know about this. I think that we should go to the police station," Frank said.

"You have a valid point, Frank. However, I want to get her out of that bastard's home before we go to the police. I knew that they were lower class, and they called themselves Pandits! I did not expect them to stoop so low," Baboo said with anger and indignation.

"Daddy, take a snack and cook off. In the meantime, let's wait until Hanoman comes home. Maybe later, we could all go over her at the Nauths' residence," Frank pleaded. he said.

Baboo thought for a while. "Okay, we will await Hanoman,"

Mangri gave him a cold cup of sugared milk with crackers. By the time he had finished eating, Hanoman arrived.

Baboo showed Hanoman the letter. Hanoman read silently. Baboo asked, "What have you gathered from that?"

"Definitely she is divorced," replied Hanoman. "I don't know why, but it happened. From the very beginning, I felt that that guy was a crook, but I did not want to say anything, for fear I may have been accused of jealousy. I do know he felt that he was too smart!"

"I think that you should go to the police," Hanoman advised with sobriety. "The police should be the ones to handle this matter. You will further have the police as evidence if they should go and find her at the Nauths' residence."

"No! I am going to get her and take her to the police," Baboo replied.

"In that case, I will go with you," Hanoman offered.

"You are welcome," said Baboo.

Baboo, Mangri, Hanoman, and Frank left their residence at 4:30 p.m. on Tuesday, December 12, 1967, to meet Lena and to inform her of her divorce. It was Baboo's intention to ask Lena to leave immediately. Baboo rode his bicycle carrying Mangri on the cycle's carrier. Hanoman and Frank rode their own bicycles. Lena was residing at the Nauths' residence, a ten-minute distance from Baboo's home.

On arrival at the Nauths' home, Baboo shouted, "Lena! Lena!" There were no doorbells to ring. The doors and windows of the Nauths' home were open. Baboo did not want to step into the yard. He therefore stood on the street and shouted Lena's name, knowing that she would definitely hear him.

Lena heard and recognized her father's voice. She came running out of the house. At the same time, Pandit Nauth came over from his shop and stood with his wife, sons, and daughters in their yard, blocking Lena's passage to her father.

Mrs. Nauth shouted, "Lena, you cannot go!"

"Yes, I have to hear what he has to say," cried Lena.

Mrs. Nauth and her daughters grabbed Lena. Baboo shouted, "Leave her alone! She has to go because she is divorced!"

Lena cried loudly, "What did you say, Daddy?"

"You are divorced, Lena. Here, I have the paper from the court. Let us go home. Leave the children and let us go," Baboo shouted.

Lena struggled to free herself. Mrs. Nauth and two of her daughters held her steady. Mrs. Nauth grabbed her hair and pulled her savagely, dragging her further into the yard. Pandit Nauth and his sons and other daughters present, armed themselves with cutlasses and sticks.

Pandit Nauth screamed, "Come and get her if you dare! We are going to make minced meat of you!" Pandit Nauth wagged his cutlass threateningly to Baboo and his companions. Frank lifted his bicycle in the air and advanced menacingly toward Pandit Nauth's war party. Pandit Nauth and his warriors stepped backward at Frank's approach.

Baboo grabbed Frank and the cycle, saying, "Frank, we haven't come here to fight. We came to get your sister, who is divorced. They are preventing her from leaving!" Frank lowered the cycle to the ground. Baboo continued in a loud voice, "Let us go to the police station, Hanoman and Frank. Let us bring the police to get her out. We will also let the cops know that they have threatened to chop us."

Baboo turned to leave. Mrs. Nauth swore and taunted Baboo, "You go to the police, we will get you, you f--- bastard!"

Mangri said to Baboo, "Take me along with you. I also want to go!"

"No! you return home, Mangri, and take care of the children!

I am not taking you with me this evening." As Baboo, Frank, and Hanoman rode off, the swearings of Mrs. Nauth echoed in their ears.

Baboo headed east, toward the police station. They had to cycle one and a half miles on the public road to reach their destination. On their way, along the roadside, they passed hundreds of people listening to a political meeting. When the cyclists had covered a distance of about half a mile, suddenly, there was a sound of a loud crash, then a second, followed by a third, and within seconds of each other.

Baboo was struck first, from behind, by the Morris Oxford motor car driven by Cholan's brother, Bilal. Mrs. Nauth was in the car. Baboo, at impact, was thrown on the bonnet of the car, that continued at high speed and struck Hanoman from behind. Hanoman was thrown into the drainage canal. The car proceeded east and struck Frank from behind. Frank was flung to the air, and he dropped in the middle of the street amid traffic. Frank received concussions of the brain, dislocation of the right shoulder, and multiple injuries and abrasions on the forehead, face, and body.

Hanoman received a broken hand, severe injuries to his feet, and several abrasions to his body. When Baboo was thrown on the hood of the car, his head struck metal, and Baboo received a fractured skull. Baboo managed to cling on as the car proceeded at about eighty miles an hour. About four hundred yards away from the point of impact, Bilal stepped heavily on the brake. Baboo was thrown off on the street. Mrs. Nauth then stepped out of the car with the crank handle and began to strike Baboo on the head with the full force of her three-hundred-pound body weight. Baboo screamed helplessly in agony. His muscles had paralyzed. Locomotion had ceased. His brains spilled on the roadway as the satanic Brahmin woman struck with psychotic frenzy. Baboo felt the pains no more! He lost consciousness and remained in coma.

Africans on the roadway screamed, panicked, and tried to render assistance. They stopped a passing taxi, ejected the passengers, and picked up Hanoman, Frank, and then Baboo, who was bleeding profusely. Hanoman was conscious, Frank delirious, and Baboo in a coma. They were rushed to the district doctor, who rendered first aid to Hanoman and Frank and stuffed Baboo's head with wads of cotton wool. The doctor referred the three injured men immediately to the Georgetown hospital.

At Vreed en hoop, the police took the men by fire launch across the Demerara River. At the Georgetown stelling, the fire ambulance picked up the injured men and took them to the Georgetown hospital.

The injured men, in their ordeal, were accompanied by two very close kinsmen from Ocean View. The Lalgees had heard of the accident and had run to Baboo's side to render assistance. The injured were immediately admitted on arrival at the public hospital. Frank and Hanoman were given painkillers for the night. Baboo was strapped to a bed and lay in deep coma. Doctors were amazed that he did not die immediately, with his smashed brain.

Forty-six hours later, at five on the morning of Thursday. December 14, Baboo, in coma, called out, "Marg! Marg! Margo!"

Frank and Hanoman, who were on beds nearby, quickly stepped to Baboo's side. He was still unconscious. Frank saw his father take a deep breath, and then he breathed no more!

Baboo had called out for Margaret, the eldest daughter remaining at home. It was his habit to wake Margaret at 5:00 a.m. to fix his breakfast and to get ready for school. Deep in his subconscious mind that fatal morning, Baboo had made his last call to awaken his daughter! It was a far call, away from home!

Hanoman and Frank burst into tears at his passing. It was not easy for them to understand, Why! Why! The sudden end of a good man! Hanoman and Frank took their discharge, against the doctor's advice, so as to make arrangements for the funeral. The factory was shut down, in respect to Baboo, on Saturday, December 16. The funeral was arranged for 4:00 p.m. on the said date. The factory blasted its siren in mournful notes that resounded around the district between the hours of three and four.

It was the biggest funeral that Uitvlugt had ever seen. Factory, field, and office workers turned out in great numbers to pay their respects to a man they had loved. All the neighboring villages mourned Baboo's passing. It was like the black week in the history of the district.

Frank fell at the graveside of his father and lost consciousness. He was taken by the police, who were there to witness the burial, to the St. Joseph's Mercy Hospital in Georgetown. The police had witnessed the postmortem of Baboo along with Mangri's brother. Baboo died from a multiple fractured skull and massive brain damages.

Lena, on hearing of the death of her father, got into a frenzied state of mind. She was convinced that she was divorced, or they would not have killed her father. She had overheard when Mrs. Nauth had called upon Bilal to drive the car and run down Baboo and his family. She had seen Mrs. Nauth and Bilal get into the car and driven off. She wanted to run and shout to her parents to get off the road, but it was already too late. Bilal had already raced off in the car.

Lena, during the night of December 12, 1967, at about midnight, looked upon Enrika and Devo sleeping. The tears streamed down her face as she made her decision. Cholan was not at home. He had not returned for the evening. She knew that he was in Georgetown. She felt that she must escape. She was afraid! They had killed her father and injured her brother-in-law. She feared they may kill her before the night was over.

She took a final look at her sleeping children, then she wriggled through the window from the third story of the building, using a torn bed spread as her rope. It was a terrifying experience for her to be dangling outside the building, but she managed to get to the ground.

The Nauth had locked and barred all the doors of the building. They had extracted the keys from the locks. Before her escape, Lena knew that her children and her were prisoners in the house of the Nauths. She desperately wanted to take the children with her, but she couldn't do that for two reasons. One, she couldn't manage to take them through the windows, and two, she feared they may cry and alert the Nauths.

In the dark, she found her way to the street. Once on the street, she stopped a passing factory worker on his way home. She cried and told her story. The African worker was shocked and sympathetic. The entire factory had heard of Baboo's sudden death. The African worker accompanied Lena to her parents' home. There she met a crowd of people keeping wake. She distinctly heard the wailing of the women. When she approached and was recognized, there ensued a loud outburst of crying.

8

Detectives started an in-depth investigation into Baboo's death. Hanoman and Frank gave written statements to the detectives confirming that there was a quarrel before the "accident" occurred. They both said that they went to the Nauths' residence to inform Lena of her divorce. They said that they accompanied Baboo because Baboo had asked them to do so. Frank told of how he was about to attack the Nauths with his raised cycle when the Nauths threatened to chop his father, and that Baboo held him back. They both said that Baboo had told the Nauths that he was going to the police station.

Mangri also gave a statement to the cops that was in agreement with that of Frank's and Hanoman's. Lena's statement to the police was the most damaging to the Nauths. Lena stated of hearing her father's call. She told of coming out into the yard and seeing her relatives on the street. Her father told her that she was divorced. Her father told her to leave there. She recounted the threats of her father-in-law, and she described how they were armed. She said her in-laws prevented her from leaving. She heard when her father said that he was going to the police station and also heard when Mrs. Nauth called upon Bilal to drive the car and run over her relatives. She said that she saw when Bilal and his mom drove off in the car.

Lena further told that she saw when Bilal and Mrs. Nauth returned with the car sometime later, and that she overheard Mrs. Nauth telling Pandit Nauth that they had struck down Baboo, his son, and his son-in-law. Mrs. Nauth, she said, told her husband that

Baboo was dead. Lena recounted how Pandit Nauth and his wife took soap, water, and rags and wiped the bloodstains off the car.

She further said that Pandit Nauth told his wife to tell the police that Baboo had thrown a stone at the windscreen of the car and broken, it. She told her father-in-law picking up a large stone from the street and placing it into the car. Lena said she remained in the house and was eventually locked in. She described how she escaped, leaving her children. Lena asked the cops to get her children. They told her that she had to petition the court.

About forty African Guyanese who had stood on the roadway and witnessed the "accident" voluntary came forward and gave statements to the police of the gruesome spectacle they had witnessed.

As a result of the investigations, Bilal and Mrs. Nauth were charged with murder in the first degree. Cholan and his eldest sister, Deva, were charged with perjury. Cholan was further charged with obtaining a divorce by false pretense. Through the investigations, the police learned that Cholan had served the divorce citation on his sister, who impersonated Lena and forged her signature.

Frank spent two weeks in the hospital, suffering with concussions and persistent headaches. Hanoman was treated and released after Baboo's burial. Mangri's home was in turmoil. Mangri had to pick the pieces up and care for the children. The main breadwinner, she realized, was gone, and she had to make the most of what Baboo had left them. Mangri was not left very well off, or badly off. She felt that she could make ends meet with frugality and with the meager earnings of Frank. Her children were young. At Baboo's death, Frank was seventeen, Margaret fifteen, Lynette thirteen, Jeanette eleven, Kenneth nine, and Radhi was six years old.

Mangri was in despair for the first few years. When Baboo was alive, he took care of all financial matters. Mangri was left to fend for herself after his death. She thanked God that the house was already paid for and that Baboo had left her no debts. As a matter of fact, at his death, there were many people who had owed Baboo. Mangri left it to the customers to pay up. She felt that if they did not pay, she would not bother, because the people were very supportive to her during the time of her disaster. Even the neighbors who were bothering her came over frequently to sympathize. Mangri felt relieved in that direction with the neighbors, that Baboo's death had brought her peace in her village!

In 1968, Cholan and his sister were tried on the perjury charges in the Supreme Court in Georgetown. The Nauths had retained two of the best criminal lawyers in Guyana and the world. They took Sir Lucknov, who was rated in the Guinness Book of Records as the criminal lawyer who had won the most murder cases in the world and was rated never to have lost any. Also, they had Mr. Keines, who was rated as Guyana's second-best criminal lawyer. Mr. Keines, because of his reputation and achievements, went on to become the Chancellor of the Judiciary.

Cholan and his sister were found guilty of perjury. The divorce that Cholan had falsely attained was set aside by the court, and the marriage was brought back legal. At the time of the court making the divorce null and void, Lena, who was presented as the plaintiff, was asked by the trial judge whether she wanted to divorce her husband because of the wrong he had done to her.

Lena's lawyer, Mr. Adamson, who was another brilliant Guyanese who later became Chief Justice of Grenada, consulted with Lena. Lena, through her lawyer, replied no, but she asked for a restraining order and the custody of the children. Lena got the restraining order, but was not granted custody, on the grounds that she was not working. The children were given into the custody of their grandfather, Pandit Nauth.

Cholan was sentenced to one year in prison, and Deva received six months.

By late 1968, Mangri, Hanoman, and Frank were not informed about the murder charges of Mrs. Nauth or Bilal, nor were they summoned to attend court. After about six months of imprisonment, Mrs. Nauth was set free. Frank had seen her sitting one day in front of her shop. Frank became suspicious and reported to Mangri and Hanoman. They went to the police precinct to inquire about the case. They were told to let the police handle their business!

On further investigations, after Frank and Hanoman befriended Corporal Soubee from the precinct, they learned that the police commandant was heavily bribed to shelve the case.

Mangri, Frank, and Hanoman, in January 1968, were approached by Mrs. Nauth's multimillionaire brother, who offered them five thousand dollars to settle the case. At the time, Frank was laid up in bed from his injuries. Hanoman, in his cool and collective way, asked the millionaire to leave in peace. He looked back and told Hanoman and Mangri that they would be sorry they didn't make the money.

Mangri, Hanoman, and Frank, after learning of the bribery to the police, went to Georgetown in November 1968 and consulted solicitor McDonnel and lawyer Ramsammy. Dr. Ramsammy was the attorney general of Guyana in the previous government. After listening to Hanoman and Frank, Dr. Ramsammy told them that in the legal records of Guyana, there was not a single conviction for murder in which the murder weapon was a motor car.

"If this case goes up to the jury as a murder case, the lawyers for the accused will rip it apart. There are no citations in the whole western hemisphere where the murder weapon was a motor car. Maybe there is a case or two in Australia, but that will not help this case!"

"Then what do you advise, Doc?" asked Frank.

"I advise that we break down the case to motor-manslaughter. Under that charge, with the large number of witnesses that you have, the driver will definitely be jailed for five years in the least. If he even received one day's jail, then you could file a lawsuit on the insurance of injuries sustained and loss of life."

Dr. Ramsammy looked at Mangri. He said, "You should think of the children you have to raise. Your husband is already dead. You need money to survive."

"Doc, I don't have much money to pay you for taking this case and for a lawsuit," Mangri said.

"You don't have to pay me anything! Do you agree that we break down the case to motor-manslaughter?" Dr. Ramsammy asked, looking at them all.

Hanoman replied, "You should know best, Doc. It's all in your hands now."

"I take that to mean that you agree!" said Dr. Ramsammy. "Okay, let's begin."

Dr. Ramsammy dialed a number. As he dialed, he whispered, "I am calling the commissioner of police, the big man himself."

The phone rang at the other end. Dr. Ramsammy said, "Could you get me the commissioner?" He waited a while, then said, "It's Dr. Ramsammy." The doctor laughed, listening to the other end, "Yes, yes, man, Mr. Commissioner, I will be there at the party tonight. Let's talk about that when we reach. I have an important matter here. I have a client here, Mrs. Mangri Arjune. Her husband was killed with a motor car in a family dispute in '67. The driver is charged with murder. What are you guys doing, ducking the case?" Dr. Ramsammy listened. He said, answering queries on the other end, "12th December, 1967... Baboo Arjune, deceased... Bilal Nauth, accused... Uitvlugt... West Coast Demerara...motor car is the weapon."

Dr. Ramsammy waited for about five minutes, then he said into the phone, "That's it. Arjune deceased. Good, I am glad the charged is still murder. Okay, listen carefully, I want the charge broken down to motor-manslaughter...yes, motor-manslaughter. The widow has many children. I want her to get money... Okay, do that for me. I owe you one. Thank you!"

Dr. Ramsammy put down the phone. He said, "The charge will be broken down. Don't be upset when you see the killer. He will be out on bail. Now, to business! I need two hundred dollars---that's all...to file the papers. I promise you that I will get him convicted. From the money you will be rewarded, you will give me twenty percent, plus the cost of the case, which will be shouldered by the insurance." He looked at them.

Hanoman said, "Agreed." Dr. Ramsammy shook their hands. Mangri gave him two hundred dollars. They bade farewell and left, with Ramsammy promising them that they will hear from him.

Frank saw Bilal sitting in front of his father's shop as he rode past the week after he met Dr. Ramsammy. Their eyes had made contact, and Bilal lowered his head. Frank felt like jumping off his bicycle and grabbing the throat of the diminutive scoundrel, but better judgment prevailed, and Frank rode on.

The preliminary inquiry of the case was held at the Leonora Magistrate's court. Because of the large number of witnesses, the inquiry took months to be concluded. The counsels for the defense tried their utmost to confuse Frank and Hanoman on the witness stand, but the two young men stood their grounds. They refused to change their statements. At the end, the magistrate concluded that there was malice aforethought. The case was bounded over to the Supreme Court. Bilal was placed on ten thousand dollars' bail and ordered to face manslaughter charge.

In the meantime, as Pandit Nauth went around the villages, practicing obeah for his heretical followers, he boasted that "the river would run dry if Bilal received one day in jail." Pandit Nauth boasted that he had the best lawyers in the country and that he had the money to buy the prosecutors. These boasts, through the grapevines, went back to the hearing of Frank, Hanoman, and Mangri. They relayed what they had heard to their counsels.

Dr. Ramsammy and his colleagues laughed and allayed the fears of Frank, Hanoman, and Mangri. The trial in the Supreme Court began on January 2, 1969. Cholan had served his sentence and was released. He attended the trial with his parents. Lena, as the star witness, accompanied Frank, Hanoman, and Mangri.

On each morning of the trial, Pandit Nauth would push his way to the front of the spectators. As he walked up the stairs of the court and into the courtroom, he would secretly deposit cloves, spices, fragrant perfume, and the petals of the hibiscus flower. He would mumble his verses and called upon the evil spirits he dealt with.

Mangri, upon noticing and smelling the relics of obeah, commented to Frank and Hanoman, "The Pandit is trying to obeah the witnesses and the judge. He is trying to make them favor Bilal, the killer!"

Frank replied, "There is no obeah that is stronger than God. Pray to God every day and you will wash away the obeah."

"But, Frank, look at the cloves and the petals on the floor. The attar smell is in the air!" she persisted.

Mangri was a devout Hindu. Frank thought that and found the answer to take his mother's mind away from fear. He said, "Ma, you would not believe me, but I also know of obeah." Mangri looked at him in disbelief.

With a twinkle in his eyes, which Mangri was too confused to detect, Frank said seriously, "Ma, don't fear Pandit Nauth and his obeah. I have been reading the Black Heart, and every morning I come here, I chant one of the verses from that great book!"

Mangri took a step backward. They were in the courthouse, awaiting the arrival of the judge. Mangri almost shouted, but checked herself in time. She stammered, "You...you...are reading that devil book? Aren't you afraid?" She looked at Frank with doubtful eyes.

"Why should I be afraid? It's only a book, and we have to win these people, come hell or high water!" Frank replied.

Mangri thought for a few seconds and replied. "I think you are right. We have to win. Your father's death cannot go unpaid!"

"That's the way to think, Ma. No obeah can affect this case. As from tomorrow, walk with a miniature photograph in your pocket of the Goddess Kali. That mother will eat up all of the obeah and also them!"

Mangri looked at Frank. She studied his face. Frank was serious. Mangri said, "Okay, Mother Kali, Mother Durga for them. I will bow down morning and night to those two mothers and beg for my reward! I will walk with their photographs in my pockets wherever I go as from this day! We will see which is more powerful, obeah or God!"

Frank was beginning to regret that he had encouraged Mangri. He realized that his mom had taken him seriously and that she would do as he had told her. He said, "Ma, take it easy. Don't get yourself too worked up! Just leave it all in the hands of God."

The bailiff saved the situation. He shouted, "All rise, His Worship, the Honorable Judge Connon Jackson, presiding!"

All stood, and the judge, clothed in his black gown and hood, stepped in, climbed the dais, and took his seat. He looked around and called upon the prosecutor.

The prosecutor began, "The state versus Bilal Nauth…" He read out his case. The judge called upon the defense. The defense outlined their course of action.

Mangri, upon hearing the outline of the defense for the accused, quietly began to pray to Mother Kali and Mother Durga and the other sisters of the nine Godheads. The judge fixed a date for the trial to begin and adjourned the case for the day.

On their way out, Cholan stepped up and spoke to Lena. Lena shrugged him off and walked on with Mangri. Cholan persisted, and Frank shoved him off, saying in anger, "Lay off her! Haven't you caused enough disasters?"

Cholan backed off. As the days went by, before the trial began, Lena started to receive numerous letters from Cholan. He wrote her saying he was sorry, he had made a mistake, she was his angel, his Sita, the darling children needed her, her family needed her. Lena would communicate the contents of these letters to Mangri. Together, they would discuss the children. Lena had told Mangri, "Ma, I want my children. I cannot live without them. I can't bear to have them growing up not knowing me and hating me!"

Mangri told her, "I know your plight, Lena! I hope that one day you will be with your children. But in the meantime, those people are beginning to win you over. They want you on their side so that they can win the case!"

"What should I do, Mom? I am divided between my love for my children and my loyalty and love for my father, who has given his life for me!" Lena would frequently burst into tears, when she discussed her children with Mangri. She was in a quandary.

The letters became more frequent. Then gifts started to arrive in the mail. She received a diamond finger ring, a golden chain, golden bracelets, beautiful dresses, large sums of money from time to time. In each gift would be a beautiful blown-up picture of her two children.

Whenever Lena looked upon the photographs of her children, she would shed tears.

Frank and Hanoman began to fear that one day before Lena had given her testimony in court, she would cross the floor and take the sides of her in-laws. Cholan wooed Lena with gusto. He pleaded his undying and eternal love to her in his mails. Mangri began to dread the mailman. Whenever she saw the mailman, she feared that he would bring disaster to her home. She feared that after Lena had read one of those mails and had seen of those incoming pictures of her children, that she would one day leave and go to her children and to Cholan and Cholan's family.

Frank and Hanoman discussed Lena's would-be reactions. Frank had told Hanoman, "Lena is constantly receiving letters and pictures of her children. I am afraid that she will go!"

Hanoman had said, "She could go if she wants, but I hope that she sticks to her story in court."

"That's what I am afraid of," replied Frank. "If she goes to them, to be able to keep her children, she would change her statement in their favor. Definitely, she cannot lead the evidence against Bilal and still remain under the same roof," Frank had said.

"Let's think about it rationally," said Hanoman. "How much damage can she do to us? How much stronger is her evidence than ours?"

"I had given the matter some thought," said Frank. "This case is no more than a murder trial. The only thing that she could withhold is that she did not hear Mrs. Nauth's instructions to Bilal, she did not see them drive off in the car, she did not hear what Mrs. Nauth told her husband when they had returned after thinking they had killed my father, and that she did not see them wiping the blood from the car. Now, those points would be relevant if it was the capital charge. If she withheld her statement of the truth, she cannot do much damage to us. We have many witnesses who would subscribe to the accident!"

"You are right, Frank," agreed Hanoman. "But those witnesses that you are talking about are so scared of Pandit Nauth's obeah!"

"I know that they are scared. I am trying to talk to them whenever I meet them in court. I am hoping and praying that they will stand behind us," Frank replied positively.

Hanoman continued, "Suppose she turns on us in court, although we know that her evidence cannot harm us much, her negation can have an adverse effect on our witnesses!"

"I agree, Hanoman! It's psychological. Our witnesses can say, 'What the hell! If the daughter goes against the father, then why should we be loyal?' We only have to hope that better judgment will prevail!" said Frank.

"Let's hope that all will go well, Frank. If she wants to go, then we cannot tie her feet and hands. It will be against the law to hold her against her will!"

The trial began, and Lena was the first witness to be called to the stand. That morning, she had left home in the company of Mangri, Frank, and Hanoman. She was extremely quiet through the journey to the High Court, in Georgetown. She did not look back at her mom when her name was called to take the witness stand. After taking the oath, the prosecutor asked, "Is your name Lena Arjune, formerly Lena Nauth?"

"Yes!"

"Were you divorced from your husband?"

Counsel for the defense shouted, "Objection, My Lord, that sort of questioning has no bearing on this case!"

"Sustained," said the judge.

The prosecutor continued, "Were you present on the evening of Tuesday, December 12, 1967, when your father, the deceased, went to your in-laws' home and called out to you?"

"Yes, sir," she answered.

"Was there a quarrel between your parents and the Nauths?"

"I can't remember!" Lena said.

"Remember you are under oath! If you lie, you will be charged with perjury!" warned the prosecutor.

"Objection, My Lord. The prosecutor is threatening the witness!"

"Sustained!" said the judge.

"If a witness does not remember, that witness does not remember! It is better to remember that to perjure!"

The counsels for the defense smiled broadly. Lena, the state witness, was playing the ball in the court of the defense.

The prosecutor continued, staring defeat in the face, "Did you hear when Mrs. Nauth called upon Bilal to drive the car and run over your parent?"

"I can't remember," Lena said quietly, with bowed head.

"Speak up!" shouted the prosecutor.

"I can't remember!" Lena said louder.

"Did you see when Bilal and Mrs. Nauth drive off in the car?"

"I can't remember!" Lena said.

"Are you suffering from amnesia or something?" angrily asked the prosecutor.

"Objection!" shouted counsel for the defense. "Prosecutor is asking witness for a medical opinion!"

"Sustained," said the judge, "Mr. Prosecutor, direct your line of questioning to the charge and not to witness physical well-being."

"Yes, My Lord!" said the prosecutor. He resumed, "Did you see when your father-in-law, Mr. Nauth, and your mother-in-law, Mrs. Nauth, were wiping away bloodstains from the motor car PW556?"

"I can't remember seeing anything, sir," Lena said meekly. The prosecutor threw his notes on the table and sat down heavily. "No more questions, My Lord!"

The judge said, "Thank you, Mr. Prosecutor." He called upon the defense, "Mr. Lucknov, Mr. Keines, your witness."

Mr. Lucknov stood and smiled, looking at Lena. He addressed the judge, "No questions My Lord, but we reserve the right to recall the witness at a later period in this case."

"Granted," said the judge. "The witness may now step down." The judge looked at Lena, and shook his head. His eyes followed Lena as she slowly walked over to the seats of the Nauths. She quietly sat down, placed her hands over her face, and burst into tears.

The Nauths were smiling and giggling. Some of them laughed too loudly. The judge said, "Quiet in this court or we will get you thrown out or charge you with contempt!"

There was quiet. Mangri was in shock. She had not expected that from Lena. Mangri went down on bended knees between the benches and began praying in earnest, asking Mothers Kali and Durga for revenge. Frank and Hanoman remained quiet. They had half expected Lena to sell out, but they had not expected the effect of her negation to be so profound on the court. The prosecutor immediately exhibited his ineptitude to cope with the dramatic. The counsels for the defense were jubilant. Mangri's counsel, Dr. Ramsammy, asked the court for a ten-minutes recess. The judge called upon the defense. The defense agreed. The court was recessed.

During the recess Dr. Ramsammy and his solicitor conferred with the prosecutor for adopting a defeatist attitude. They reminded him that it was not a murder trial and one witness's withdrawal from the state cannot do much damage to the entire case. Dr. Ramsammy and Mr. McDonnel, the solicitor, pledged their support to the prosecutor and reminded him that they were there on behalf of the plaintiffs. They promised to pass him notes as the trial continued. They told him that they wanted a conviction because they would represent the plaintiffs, also, in the lawsuit that would follow. The prosecutor promised to do his best.

The court resumed. The next witness was called. Hanoman took the stand, then Frank. The defense tried to shake Hanoman and Frank, but these two young men stood like bulwarks, unshaking, unmoved during the most rigorous cross-examinations by two attorneys who were world renowned.

Mr. Lucknov, exhibited his flamboyance and his Guinness-glorified fame in his cross-examination to Frank. He had said, "You told the court that when you heard the first impact, you turned around and saw the car approaching you in a northeasterly direction. I am saying that you lied to this court, because the street runs in an east/west direction!"

Frank had remained quiet, waiting for Mr. Lucknov's question. "From what direction did you see motor car PW556 approaching you?"

"Northeasterly!" answered Frank.

"Is the road running east to west?"

"Yes, sir, but it is very wide!"

"Did you see the car swerve?"

"No, sir!"

"Then you are lying!" he shouted.

"Maybe you were there, sir, and you saw it all!"

The court resounded with laughter. Mr. Lucknov was angry. The judge banged his gavel. "Quiet in this court." He did not admonish Frank.

Dr. Ramsammy stood and addressed the court. The judge acknowledged him, "My Lord, the witness had said that the road is very wide and it also runs in an east to west direction. When he heard the impact and he turned, he could have missed when the car had swerved to the southern side of the road. All he saw was the car crossing the road from the southern side to the northern side where he was impacted. It all happened in seconds, because of the speed of the car. If the point is not understood, I am inviting the court to inspect the street at the point of impact!"

Dr. Ramsammy sat. The judge asked the defense lawyers if they would like to inspect the street. They declined. The judge then clarified the point. "The witness has said that he saw motor car PW556 moving from the southern side of the street to the northern side where it impacted him on his bicycle. Any objection, Mr. Lucknov?"

"Agreed, My Lord!" replied Mr. Lucknow.

"You may proceed with your cross-examination, Mr. Lucknov," ordered the judge.

"No more questions, sir," said Mr. Lucknov.

The judge looked at his watch. It was 3:45 p.m. He said, "This court is adjourned until 9:00 a.m. tomorrow."

The spectators filed out. Mangri, Frank, and Hanoman left. Frank looked behind as he walked. Cholan was holding Lena's hand, leading her out of the courthouse. His other relatives were close around her. They were all talking and smiling with her.

Although Mangri had heard the evidences of Frank and Hanoman, she was still extremely angry at Lena's betrayal. Mangri went home and fasted. She sincerely prayed for revenge. She called upon God to let her enemies suffer in the same way as she had suffered to let her enemies experience the same feelings that she had experienced at the sudden killing of her husband and companion.

Mangri was thirty-nine years old when Baboo died. She never remarried, nor had she ever entertained the idea of a second marriage. She dedicated herself to her children. She did not look upon the face of another man with sexual fancies.

The trial climaxed in January 1970. Sessions ran into sessions. There were many witnesses-hospital attendants, doctors, pathologists, police, and eyewitnesses. At the end, Bilal was found guilty of motor-manslaughter. He was sentenced to five years' imprisonment, with no parole. The river did not run dry, as Pandit Nauth had predicted, nor did any of the witnesses die from mysterious deaths that could have been attributed to obeah.

A few weeks after the sentencing of Bilal, the lawsuit was brought up in the High Court. Dr. Ramsammy won against the insurance company of the motor car that Bilal had driven. Mangri received fifty thousand dollars; Frank, ten thousand; Hanoman, five thousand, and each of the minor children were also rewarded sums of money that were held in trust of the court until they attained the age of eighteen.

Lena could not have returned to her mother's home any longer. She had her conscience to contend with and the people to face. In the eyes of the people, she was a traitor! In 1970, Lena gave birth to her second son, whom Cholan and her named Bobby. Bobby was born at the home of the Nauths.

Gradually, after Bobby's birth, the Nauths returned to their routine toward Lena. The gifts were withdrawn, and Cholan started staying away from Lena. Cholan and Lena bitterly fought. During one of the skirmishes between Cholan and Lena, Lena was so badly beaten and bruised, she had to be hospitalized.

When Bobby was two years old, Cholan told Lena that he was taking the children to see Santa in Georgetown. It was the Christmas season of 1972.

"I want to accompany you guys! You can't take care of all three of them by yourself!" Lena had said.

"Yes! I could manage," replied Cholan. "They are little darlings when they are with me! Don't bother, all will be well!"

"What time would you return home this evening?" Lena asked.

"Why? We will be here by about 5:00 p.m.? said Cholan.

Lena bathed and dressed the kids. She fed them and watched as they drove off in the car with Cholan's younger brother at the wheel.

Lena wished her children goodbye and hoped they would be safe for the day!

C h a p t e r

9

Lena had hoped that her children would see Santa and would enjoy the day with their dad. She also wished that she had 'been with them. She knew that if she insisted to go, it would have been another brawl between Cholan and herself, and she would have ended up to be the wounded party. On the other hand, she did not want to spoil Christmas for her children. She therefore backed down and let Cholan have his way.

However, all that day, she was very anxious. When 5:00 p.m. had passed and Cholan did not show up with the children, she became restless. She watched the clock as the minutes ticked by. Then it was dusk, and no Cholan! Then night fell, and Lena heard a car drive into the yard.

She rushed to the door and shouted joyfully. Then she saw neither Cholan nor the children emerging from the car! "Where are they, Chabbie! Where are my children?" She rushed to the car. It was empty except for Chabbie, the driver. Lena was frantic and scared.

Chabbie emerged from the car, looked at Lena, and smiled. He started to walk. Lena ran and grabbed him by the shoulder. She shook him. "Where are my children, Chabbie?" she pleaded. "Please tell me."

Chabbie turned, looked at her streaming face, and happily said, "They are gone, bitch, gone! I took them to the airport. They flew out to Canada!"

"You are lying!" She held Chabbie with both hands on his shoulder. She hysterically shook him. "You are lying! You are lying!" she screamed.

Her screams brought Pandit and Mrs. Nauth from the house running. Pandit Nauth spoke, "You are back, Chabbie! Have they left safely?"

"Yes, Dad! They flew out safely."

Mrs. Nauth addressed Lena, "Bitch, your children and Cholan are gone! They have left for Canada! When he arrives there, he will marry his Georgetown sweetheart, who is a Canadian resident. Bitch, this is the end for you!"

Lena couldn't believe her ears! She felt that she was dreaming! This wasn't happening! She was asleep!

Pandit Nauth's voice woke her up. "You have one hour to leave. Grab what you can and go. There is nothing left here for you now!"

Lena walked as if in a daze. If the ground could open, she would willingly go down! This couldn't be! She went against her parents because of her children! And now this! With tears blinding her eyes, she packed a shoulder bag with whatever came to her grasp. She staggered out of the house, moaning to herself. The jeers and laughter of the Nauths reverberated in her ears!

Where should she go? Her mother's home was half a mile away, but could she go there? No! How could she face her mother and brothers and sisters after what she had done? Would they forgive her? Had they forgiven her? No! She did not want to find out!

Oh god, when will this stop! When will my punishment cease! Lena moaned.

She took a cab to Georgetown. As she traveled, her mind began to clear. She felt devastated, but she had to think! What should she do? As she crossed Demerara River with the ferry Makouria, she thought of suicide. She walked to the rails on the bow of the ferry and contemplated climbing the rails and plunging into the fast-flowing murky water of the treacherous river's mouth. She looked toward the Atlantic Ocean, the wide and endlessly sprawling water. She felt alone, very lonely. It was as if she was mesmerized by the openness, the vastness of the unending waters. She started to pray. She called upon the name of Jesus, Rama, Mohammad, and all the deities she could remember.

As she prayed, Lena began to experience a sudden calm in her body---a sudden peace. She began to realize that should she commit suicide, she would never be able to see her children again. But on the other hand, if she lived, she realized that there would be hope. She felt that she had done no wrong, and that if she prayed from the bottom of her heart, that one day God would answer her prayers and she would be with her children again. Lena dried her tears and remained calm.

At Georgetown, she hailed a cab and went to an old friend that she had once known. Mrs. Bacchus was a widow. Lena and Cholan had once rented an apartment in Mr. Bacchus's house, in Kitty, Greater Georgetown. Mrs. Bacchus was aware of Cholan's previous ill treatment of Lena, and she had advised Lena to divorce Cholan. Mrs. Bacchus, in her late fifties, was childless. She had looked upon Lena as her daughter.

When Lena rapped on her door on that December evening in 1972 and Mrs. Bacchus had opened up to Lena, she instantly realized on seeing Lena standing there alone, that something was desperately wrong. Lena started crying when she saw Mrs. Bacchus. Mrs. Bacchus opened her arms, embraced and comforted Lena. She literally carried Lena into the house, for Lena, with suspense and anguish throughout the day, had grown weak and became limp as she fell into the loving hands of the motherly Mrs. Bacchus.

"Come, my child! Don't weep! Whatever your problems are, God is greater! Don't give up, just pray, and all will be well for you one day. Your world cannot be dark all the time, Lena. God is just, and He will give you your reward one day!"

Between sobs, Lena said, "Aunt Bacchus, it is terrible. Cholan had escaped today to Canada, stealing my children away from me. He said he was taking them to Georgetown to see Santa Claus, but instead, he took them to Canada! Aunty, it's terrible! I can't bear it! I felt like taking my life!" Lena sobbed hysterically in the arms of Mrs. Bacchus.

Mrs. Bacchus pressed Lena's head to her bosom as she led Lena to a sofa. She gently patted Lena on the back of the head, whispering between pats, "Don't cry, my child! Don't cry! It is dark now for you, but Allah will be on your side. I will go to mosque and pray for you. Allah will give you justice one day, my child! Don't give up hope! Don't ever think of suicide! Only a coward takes her own life, and you are no coward! You have faced a lot, and a little more would not kill you!"

Lena's crying subsided. Mrs. Bacchus gently moved back Lena's head and looked at her tearstained face. She said, "That's a good girl. Crying and mopping around would make you sick. You have to be strong to live to meet the challenges of this world. I will have you here. Boarding and lodging will be free. I have no children, and now God has sent me a daughter. We will face this problem together. Time will solve everything. Relax some more, then take a shower. I will get you a hot cup of tea and something to eat! After shower and your meal, go to bed. We will talk tomorrow."

Lena thanked Mrs. Bacchus. The good lady accompanied Lena to the bathroom door. She said, "Go in and shower, and don't lock the door. I want to make sure that you are okay!" Mrs. Bacchus looked at Lena sternly but lovingly. Lena hugged and kissed her on the cheek. Mrs. Bacchus smiled. The tears welled in her eyes. Lena stepped into the bathroom.

Lena resided at Mrs. Bacchus's residence from December 1970 to the year 1980. She secured a job as a telex operator and stenographer at the offices of Guyana Store in Water Street, Georgetown. She worked and she prayed that she may hear of her children. But no word came.

She visited the Canadian High Commission in Georgetown and reported her story, but she got no help from that direction. She often asked Guyanese visitors from Canada whether they had heard of Cholan and her children, but got no encouraging news either. Lena lived in hope. Hope kept her alive. Hope sustained and nurtured her. Prayers also kept her alive, and Mrs. Bacchus was a mother to her.

In 1973, the first disaster struck the Nauth family. Mangri was persistent in her prayers. Lena devoutly worshipped God. Some

Hindus believe that if someone does you severe wrong, that within fourteen years after that grave wrong was done to you, your enemy will begin to suffer for the sin or crime he has committed against you.

Retributions began to step in, in 1973; the Nauths began to pay back dearly. Whether God has stepped in to avenge Baboo's death, no one knows! Whether the prayers of Mangri and Lena were answered, no one knows! But the retribution of the Nauths were devastating and nerve rending! The obeah of Pandit Nauth could not have stopped the price the Nauth family paid!

In 1973, one of the younger sons of the Nauths fell suddenly ill and died. He was ten years old at the time of his death. He was diagnosed with lymphatic tumor of the brain and died within a month of his diagnosis. The death of this child was beyond the sanity of Mrs. Nauth. She cried for weeks and months after the funeral of her child until she became a nervous wreck.

By the end of 1974, Mrs. Nauth contracted Parkinson's disease. It wrecked her nervous system to such an extent that she was literally unable to feed or wash herself. In 1974, Bilal was released from prison. He immediately joined the Ramakrishna movement and rose to be the leader of that organization in Guyana.

Bilal chanted "Hare Rama, Hare Krishna," and prayed for the forgiveness of his sins and the salvation of his soul. Bilal danced in the streets to the beating of drums and the chiming of cymbals, leading his innocent followers into a life similar to the Davidian fanaticism. He collected, over the years, huge sums of money and converted the same to his own use. He married one of the converted sisters of the organization, and he lived in physical comfort and luxury at the expense of the Ramakrishna movement. In his mind, however, Bilal anguished everlastingly. His mind was tortured and disturbed, as he survived to watch the demise of his parents, brothers, and sisters.

In 1980, Bilal's third brother migrated to the United States of America, and he joined the military. He was stationed in Florida. His name was Bharat. During the Miami uprising, Bharat was murdered and chopped to pieces, beyond recognition.

In the years, between 1975 and 1976, Bilal's entire family migrated to the United States. On their arrival in the States, the husbands of his six sisters divorced their wives and married other women.These former brothers-in-law of Bilal's had learned of Baboo's murder, and they were witnesses to the beginnings of the retributions. These men were terribly afraid. They feared that should they remain married to the sisters of Bilal, then as members of the family they would also suffer in the retributions. They sensed that God was angry with Pandit Nauth, and they did not want to face the wrath of God! They felt that they were innocent of the murder of Baboo, and to continue to be innocent, they had to break their ties with the family of the Nauths. They divorced their wives! They broke clean of the family.

By 1980, Frank had relented. His anger was appeased. He prayed sincerely to God to stop the wrath on the doorsteps of the Nauths. As the disaster struck the Nauths, the grapevine brought the news to Baboo's family. Frank, by 1980, thought that his father's death was avenged and pleaded in his prayers to God to stop the destruction of the Nauths.

Frank, accompanied by his wife, visited Lena. The ice melted between them, and Baboo's family was reunited. Mangri was happy to have Lena back. Each of her brothers and sisters welcomed her back. Not long after Lena rejoined her mother and brothers and sisters, she received a cable. It was from her daughter and eldest child, Enrika. The cable read, "Mommy, we need you. Daddy is dead." It gave an address and a phone number. Lena had received the cable on her job at Guyana stores.

Cholan, through other Guyanese immigrants to Canada, had kept track of Lena. On his dying bed, he had told his children of their mother's whereabouts and had given them the address of her workplace. When Cholan had died, Enrika cabled her mother, the woman her brothers and her had grown to forget. She cried and asked for permission to go home. Lena traveled to her mother's home to see Mangri and her brothers and sisters. She wanted to discuss the news with them. She wanted them to be a part of her joy and to realize why she had given up so much for her children!

Everyone was elated. Frank advised her to take the cable the next morning to the Canadian High Commission in Georgetown. "I will go with you!" volunteered Mangri.

"Walk with your passport," Frank told her, "in case they grant you the visa."

Lena was afraid. "Ma, it's eight years now since I last saw those children! I am afraid to meet them!"

"Why are you afraid?" asked Frank's wife, Marguerita, "They are your kids! They have only grown a bit older!"

"I wouldn't know them," explained Lena. "I haven't seen any photographs of them for eight years. I can only remember them when they were very small!"

"Don't bother," said Marguerita. "Kids grow up, and one day they will understand what really happened!"

"Don't be afraid to meet them," encouraged Frank. "They do not know the truth, and they have been filled with what was fed to them by the Nauths! You are their mom! Go to them. They need you now!"

"What about money? Would you have enough for passage and for foreign exchange, that is Canadian currencies?" asked Marguerita.

"I have some savings. Should I get a visa, I will sell some of my belongings, like household effects, to raise more cash," Lena replied.

"Don't be afraid to speak to the counselors at the High Commission," advised Frank. "Walk with the children's birth certificates and your marriage certificate to prove affinity. The officials will ask for those documents," Frank told her.

Lena received a Canadian visa the following day. She was extremely happy. At long last, she would be reunited with her children! Mangri accompanied her to the ticket office of the British West Indian Airlines, and Lena booked a one-way flight to Toronto. When she received the airline ticket in her hands, she wanted to jump for joy with thought that she would be free, at last, to have her children to herself.

For the first time, she thought of Cholan's death. She knew that he was sick, sick in his brains, and that he was evil. She had tolerated him, after the murder of Baboo, solely for her children's sake. She had withstood his tortures, his brutality, and his insanity for the preservation and for the betterment of her children. She had always hoped that Cholan would change for the better, but instead, her last years with Cholan was tantamount to living in hell with all the demons molesting her.

After Cholan had deserted her with the children, Lena took her suffering calmly. Mrs. Bacchus kept speaking to her and smothering her mind with motherly love and affection. Lena had bided her time with prayers, attending business class, reading, and working. She filled her days with long hours of work and her nights with reading. For years she was restless and sleepless. The nights, for her, were unending. She would lay in bed and stare into the gloomy darkness that surrounded her.

After the third year of sleeplessness, she began to take valium to enhance sleep, but alas! Lena's eyes had kept peering into the darkness, until she began to discern, in her mind's eye, the faces of her smiling children. By the end of 1975, Lena became a somnambulist. She would often, in her trance-like sleep, walk to the door and try to open it to let in her stranded babies. Mrs. Bacchus, who was a very light sleeper, had often caught Lena sleepwalking. To prevent Lena innocently harming herself, Mrs. Bacchus moved her sleeping cot in the passageway between Lena's room and the exit door of her house.

Mrs. Bacchus took Lena to many doctors, who counseled and prescribed various medications. Nothing was of much help to her. By 1977, Lena's bed began to move in the dark. She told Mrs. Bacchus someone was lifting her bed off the floor and slamming it down to the floor again. She complained that someone was lifting her bed and slamming it to the roof while she was on it. She told of her bed and the things in her room that moved about of their own accord. She narrated stories of her dresses and underwear marching around the room! She heard her radio beginning to play without her turning it on!

Mrs. Bacchus listened to Lena's stories. She had never heard or seen what Lena had described. She slept outside of Lena's door, but she never heard any strange sound except that of Lena's movements.

Mrs. Bacchus took Lena to see the bush-doctors, who also gave her their concoctions, but alas, they were of no help to her!

The best medicine for her was when Frank visited her in 1980. From then onward, her recovery was miraculous. By the time she had heard from Enrika, Lena was in almost perfect health. When she had received the airline ticket to Canada, her blood circulated faster around her body, rejuvenating her! When she boarded the plane en route to Canada, she was healthy, strong, brave, and ready to face the adventure ahead of her.

She journeyed into the unknown to meet her children, the children whom she had birthed and always loved, but whom she was cheated of rearing all by herself. When she boarded the plane, at the Timehri International Airport in Guyana, she prayed to God to guide her path and to remove the obstacles that may still lay between her and her children.

Upon her arrival at the Canadian Airport, Lena looked for the children she once knew, but she recognized none of the faces at which she stared. Suddenly, she heard her name called. "Mommy, Mother, Lena." She looked and saw the most beautiful slim girl gracefully striding between two tall young men as they approached her.

They had recognized their mother. She looked at their faces. She recognized her big eyes in Enrika's and instantly knew that they were her children. She saw the imprint of her father upon the features of the boys and felt assured that they were her children. They stopped a few feet away and looked at her. She stopped and opened her arms. Bobby, ten, and Devo, fifteen, moved toward her and held her, shedding tears of joy at the meeting, in togetherness and the renewal of acquaintances.

On Lena's behalf, it was tears for finding her long-lost children. She didn't know what to say! She asked, "How are you guys keeping? How are you, Bobby, my little baby?" It was the wrong beginning. Bobby took offense. He unhooked her hand and said, "I am not a baby! I am ten years old!"

"All right! I am sorry! How are you, big man?" she asked again. They all laughed. She admired them. They were brave kids.

Enrika said, "Mommy, we missed you, but where were you when I needed you?"

Defensively, Lena replied, "Didn't your father tell you! Can't you remember what he did eight years ago? You were old enough, Enrika, to have understood what he did and to explain to your brothers!"

They had reached Enrika's car. They opened the door for her. Devo got behind the wheel. Lena was scared, but he drove carefully. Enrika insisted, pursuing her antagonism, "Yes, Mommy, where were you when we needed you?"

Lena felt that it was better to hit the iron while it was hot. She replied to Enrika, and for all the ears, "Didn't he lie to you also? Did he fill your heads with lies? Didn't he tell you how he deserted me in Guyana and stole you away from me? Didn't he...?"

"Stop it, Mommy! Stop it! Don't say anything bad about Daddy!" shrieked Enrika.

"I am not saying anything bad about your father, Enrika. I am merely answering your question. You are trying to blame me when your father is the one to be blamed! Do you know that he did not divorce me, that I was legally married to him up to the last moment he drew breath?"

They looked at her, opening their big eyes with total shock and surprise. The car swerved, Lena shouted, "Devo, look where you are driving! Enough of this conversation! We will talk when we get to where we are going!"

There was silence. Bobby snuggled into Lena's arms.

It was a small apartment with two bedrooms that the children occupied. The rent was paid for by the state. Enrika slept in one room, and her two brothers in the other. There was a tiny sitting room, dining room, and kitchen. The furniture in the apartment were worn with constant use and uncaring. The paint peeled from the walls in various places, and there were several dirty blotches visible in the rooms and kitchen.

Lena learned that Cholan had been ill and laid up in bed for about eighteen months. Enrika took care of her father and brothers. She did the cleaning, cooking, and housekeeping. She was not able to fully cope with all the responsibilities. Cholan was diagnosed with lymphatic tumors in his brain. He was treated with chemotherapy, but the treatment only prolonged his suffering. It did not eradicate the tumor completely from his brain. Unluckily for Cholan, chemotherapy did not make his brain tumors malignant.

Enrika told her mother that her father died calling upon the name of Lena and praying for her forgiveness.

Enrika was an embittered child. She blamed her mother for her ill treatment and child abuse at the hand of her father. Lena was shocked as Enrika recounted her life and that of her brothers from the time they had last seen their mother. As the ice melted between mother and daughter on the night of Lena's arrival in Canada, Enrika held her mother's hand as they lay in bed together, and tearfully she filled in her mother with the part of her life that Lena had not known.

She said, "Two weeks after we arrived in Canada, Daddy met and befriended a Canadian citizen of Trinidadian birth. A month later, he married her!"

"What? How could he have done that? We were not divorced! He committed bigamy!"

"Well, he did that!" said Enrika. "She bore him a son. The boy is seven years old, but he was born with a physical defect! He has paralysis, but he is a loving kid!"

"My god! He has brought another child into this world through his sinful ways, to suffer!" Lena surprised herself by uttering aloud her thought.

"Mommy, refrain from saying anything bad about him. He was both our mother and father for eight years when you were not here!"

"I was not here not because of my own free will, and you know that!" Lena replied sharply.

"I am sorry, Mommy!" Enrika apologized. "Our stepmother was mean to us. She cared only for her child. She hated us when we complained to Daddy!"

"That's expected. She was probably bitter that her poor child was born disabled while you guys are physically fit," Lena consoled.

"Maybe! But she was just plain mean to us!"

Lena turned and hugged Enrika. She whispered, "My baby! My poor baby!"

Devo and Bobby were asleep on cushions on the floor in the room. Bobby had cuddled near Lena. He brought a cushion in the room, threw it on the ground, and instantly fell asleep. Devo had followed his younger brother and done the same. Devo did not speak much. He listened to his mother speaking to Enrika until he dozed off.

"What about school?" Lena asked. "Are you guys attending school?"

"Yes! We are all in school, but Daddy's illness had affected us very much. We were frequently absent!" replied Enrika.

"Okay, from now onwards. You guys will attend regularly. After high school I want you guys to go on to college. I want each of you to be able to help yourselves. Education is the way to success!" encouraged Lena.

"We all like school, and I will try to do my best. Devo and Bobby also love school," Enrika said.

"I am glad to hear that. Now how do you guys stand with money?" Lena asked.

"Daddy left us nothing. We receive dole from the state. He was too ill to work. When he died, his wife left with her son and returned to her parents. We were left to fend for ourselves!"

"How did he treat you guys? Was he good to you?"

"Frequently he mistreated us. He often listened to his wife's complaints and beat us. Many times he locked me in my room!" Enrika began to weep.

Lena turned and comforted her. Enrika sobbed. "He was crazy, Mum! The cancer was eating his brains!

"Where did he sleep?" Lena asked.

"He slept on the couch in the hall," answered Enrika. She turned on her tummy, and her body shook with her boisterous sobs. Lena patted her on the shoulder, quietly weeping herself.

"I am sorry I asked," she whispered.

"It's all right!" Enrika sobbed.

Lena cursed under her breadth. She wished his soul to languish in the fiery hell until eternity! To Enrika, she crooned, "My poor baby! You had a hard time, but don't be afraid, Mommy is here now. I will take care of you."

They talked until they dozed off.

The following day, Lena took the children individually to their schools and met their teachers. She introduced herself as their mother and asked that she should be contacted whenever they were absent from school. She left the children's phone number with the teachers.

On the third day, Lena thoroughly cleaned and rearranged the apartment. On the fourth day of her arrival in Canada, she went job hunting. She took along her certificates and passports. She was lucky! She got a job at a hospital as a receptionist. Her experience with the telephone and her Pitman's qualifications were assets. She was told to report for work on the following Monday.

Lena used the weekend to get acquainted with her growing children. She took them clothing and food shopping. They bought new curtains for the apartment. They took their breakfasts at nearby restaurants. Together they cooked and shared dinner in the apartment.

She refrained from asking about their father. They avoided speaking about him. They sought common and mutual grounds for conversations. They prevented antagonisms among themselves, and they began to build a relationship of understanding, trust, and love. Lena watched her children grow to adulthood. Like her mother, she waited and lived to see her children grow up into adulthood.

Enrika married when she was twenty-one. After she gave birth to her second child, disaster struck the family again. Enrika was diagnosed with lymphatic tumor on her brain. She is presently receiving chemotherapy, and the doctors have said that her chances for survival are fifty-fifty.

Pandit Nauth divorced his wife in the Bronx, New York, and married an American. Shortly after his marriage, Pandit Nauth suffered a massive heart attack. Parkinson's disease continues to ravage the nervous system of Mrs. Nauth.

Mangri is sincerely praying for the revival of her granddaughter and for the salvation of Mrs. Nauth. Mangri told her children that she often dreamt of Baboo. She said he is weeping for his granddaughter. Frank is praying for the retribution to stop! He is trying to understand why the sins of the parents fall upon the children.

EPILOGUE

Everyone in the Arjune family sincerely wants Enrika to live. Each member of the family is praying for her well-being. 'Although Enrika is not known by most of the family, they know that she was the first of the third generation to bring forth to the fourth. The Arjunes hope that Enrika would live to see her two daughters grow up to be ladies who will give birth to the fifth generation of Arjune's bloodline! Sadly, Enrika died in December 1992. Long live Enrika! Long live the name of her grandfather, Baboo Arjune!

9 781962 733526